"What if I asked you to marry me?"

She stared at him. "That's a joke and I'm not even going to dignify it with a response."

"Why not? I'm dead serious." He rested his hands on lean hips as he met her gaze.

Her heart was pounding. She couldn't think straight.

"Marriage?" She held out her hands, a helpless gesture. "I don't even know how to respond to that."

"How much will it take to convince you that I've never been more serious in my life? You're the answer to my prayer. What will it cost for you to marry me?"

She said the first thing that popped into her mind. "A million dollars."

"Done," Jason said without hesitation.

Dear Reader,

I love kids. From the time I was a little girl, if someone in the neighborhood had a baby I was glued to their side. I'm the middle child of six and helped with the younger ones, who were almost as big as me. These days, my definition of family isn't just those with whom I share DNA, it includes the people who touch my heart and become part of my life.

Maggie Shepherd, the heroine of *Marrying the Virgin Nanny,* was abandoned as a baby at the Good Shepherd Home for Children. The nuns and kids there became her family and she'd do anything to protect them, including marrying Jason Garrett, the wealthy boss who makes her an offer she can't refuse.

Jason has his own family problems. He needs a nanny and is dealing with a controlling father who keeps getting marriage wrong. When Jason meets Maggie, he'd do anything to make sure she's there for his infant son— anything except fall in love.

For me, the only thing better than holding a baby is writing about one, especially the littlest matchmaker who brings Jason and Maggie together. I hope you enjoy their story and look for the next two books in THE NANNY NETWORK series.

Happy reading!

Teresa Southwick

MARRYING THE VIRGIN NANNY

TERESA SOUTHWICK

Silhouette

SPECIAL EDITION®

Published by Silhouette Books

America's Publisher of Contemporary Romance

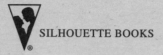

SILHOUETTE BOOKS

ISBN-13: 978-0-373-65442-0
ISBN-10:   0-373-65442-1

Recycling programs
for this product may
not exist in your area.

MARRYING THE VIRGIN NANNY

Visit Silhouette Books at www.eHarlequin.com

Printed in U.S.A.

Books by Teresa Southwick

Silhouette Special Edition

The Summer House #1510
  "Courting Cassandra"
*Midnight, Moonlight &
  Miracles* #1517
It Takes Three #1631
~*The Beauty Queen's Makeover* #1699
At the Millionaire's Request #1769
§§*Paging Dr. Daddy* #1886
‡*The Millionaire and the M.D.* #1894
‡*When a Hero Comes Along* #1904
‡*Expecting the Doctor's Baby* #1924
‡‡*Marrying the Virgin Nanny* #1960

Silhouette Books

The Fortunes of Texas
Shotgun Vows

Silhouette Romance

*Wedding Rings and
  Baby Things* #1209
The Bachelor's Baby #1233
A Vow, a Ring, a Baby Swing #1349
The Way to a Cowboy's Heart #1383
And Then He Kissed Me #1405
With a Little T.L.C. #1421
The Acquired Bride #1474
Secret Ingredient: Love #1495
The Last Marchetti Bachelor #1513
**Crazy for Lovin' You* #1529
**This Kiss* #1541
**If You Don't Know by Now* #1560
**What If We Fall in Love?* #1572
Sky Full of Promise #1624
†*To Catch a Sheik* #1674
†*To Kiss a Sheik* #1686
†*To Wed a Sheik* #1696

††*Baby, Oh Baby* #1704
††*Flirting with the Boss* #1708
††*An Heiress on His
  Doorstep* #1712
§*That Touch of Pink* #1799
§*In Good Company* #1807
§*Something's Gotta Give* #1815

*The Marchetti Family
**Destiny, Texas
†Desert Brides
††If Wishes Were…
§Buy-a-Guy
~Most Likely To…
§§The Wilder Family
‡The Men of Mercy Medical
‡‡The Nanny Network

TERESA SOUTHWICK

lives with her husband in Las Vegas, the city that
reinvents itself every day. An avid fan of romance
novels, she is delighted to be living out her dream of
writing for Silhouette Books.

To Charles Griemsman, who is simply a joy to work with.
You're the best!

Chapter One

Margaret Mary Shepherd had never been the sort of woman men undressed with their eyes.

But if Maggie had to pick someone for that particular job based solely on looks, Jason Garrett would be right at the top of her list. Dark curly hair and eyes the color of coal complemented the brooding look he no doubt used from the boardroom to the bedroom.

Standing in the doorway of his penthouse condo just off the Las Vegas Strip, Maggie listened to the wail of an infant and knew the exact moment the decibel level went up. The man winced, an expression that was perilously close to panic and put him on the fast track to fear. It also told her that what she looked like underneath her crisp denim jeans and blue turtleneck sweater wasn't even on his priority list.

"I very much hope that you're Ms. Shepherd from The Nanny Network," he said.

"I am."

"Thank God." He opened the door wider for her to enter. "Ginger Davis promised that you would be here within the hour."

"She said it was an emergency, Mr. Garrett."

He ran his fingers through his hair and from the looks of it, that wasn't the first time. Quite a tall man, he forced her to look up. His wrinkled white dress shirt with sleeves rolled up and recklessly loosened striped tie only added to his potent masculinity.

"I need a nanny," he said. Desperate need, judging by the ragged expression on his face. "Ginger assured me that infants are your specialty—"

An enraged, tiny-baby wail came from somewhere nearby. "Right on cue. That must be yours."

"My son, yes."

"I'll just go—"

"Wait." He glanced in the direction of the cry. "According to your employer you are the very best at what you do, but I'd like some confirmation."

The baby's distress was making Maggie want to tell him what he could do with his confirmation. "Isn't that why you contacted The Nanny Network? The agency has made its reputation by conducting thorough personnel background and qualification checks. Peace of mind is part of the service."

"I haven't had a chance to check out Ginger Davis and The Nanny Network the way I'd like. But I'm not hiring 'Ginger and Company.' You're the one who will be taking care of my son. The circumstances I find myself in—"

"What is your situation, Mr. Garrett?"

"I've had three nannies since my son was born and he's only a month old, born December eleventh. I need someone to care for him, someone I can trust."

The cry increased in pitch and urgency and Maggie couldn't stand it.

"Look, Mr. Garrett, I'm not sure what your problem is that

makes it a challenge for you to keep a nanny, but the job interview can wait." She turned in the direction of the crying.

"Hold on a second—"

"Not while that baby is upset."

As she hurried down the hall with the man hot on her heels, Maggie's impression of his home was understated sophistication and simple elegance that probably cost a bundle. The guy was loaded, some kind of genius developer sensation. And what did any of that matter to the tiny infant who was clearly distressed about something?

She found the nursery and hurried over to the crib. The infant was on his back, thank goodness. His little face was red and the desperate cry was constant, high pitched. His hands and feet were going a mile a minute and his little mouth quivered in the way babies did that could just break your heart.

Without hesitation, she reached in and scooped him into her arms. "Oh my goodness, sweetheart," she cooed. She lifted him against her chest and rubbed his back, making him feel as secure as possible. "It's going to be okay. I promise."

She pressed him close and gently swayed, the movement coming automatically. When he'd calmed enough, she settled him into the bend of her elbow, then took his tiny hand in hers and brushed his palm with her thumb. The intensity of the cries diminished until the sound was more like a cat's meow, one that was telling her off big time for letting the situation deteriorate to such a low.

"I know, sweetheart. You're absolutely right. The conditions here are deplorable and completely intolerable. But things are looking up." She glanced at Jason Garrett who was watching her through narrowed eyes.

"I wasn't finished talking to you." He wasn't accustomed to losing control of a situation.

"I was finished talking to you until this little one is sufficiently reassured that his needs will be met." She cuddled the child close. Smiling down she asked, "What's his name?"

"Brady." He moved close. "Brady Hunter Garrett." Tentatively brushing a finger over the downy dark fuzz on the child's head, he smiled.

Maggie's stomach quivered and pitched. He'd been all brooding darkness until he looked at his son. It was an expression so tender and loving her heart quivered and pitched, too.

"It's a good, strong name." She continued to caress the tiny palm as she said, "It's nice to meet you, Brady Hunter Garrett."

"Are you always so take-charge?" he asked.

"Are you always so long-winded?"

"What does that mean?" he demanded, the brooding look back.

"Brady's needs come before yours."

"Not when my need is to make sure he's safe," Garrett snapped.

"It's easy to see why you go through nannies like napkins at a car wash."

"I don't have to explain myself to you. I'm the employer; you're the employee."

"Not yet. If you can interview me, I should be extended the same courtesy to decide whether or not I want to work for you."

"Do you screen all potential employers?"

"This is the first time."

Maggie wasn't sure why she was doing it now except something was weird here. Her specialty was infants from birth to six weeks. Go in, stabilize the situation, so new mom could get her sea legs and some rest, get out before she, Maggie, fell in love with the child and couldn't leave without breaking her heart. Ginger Davis, owner of The Nanny Network, had always placed her in work situations with couples—husband and wife or man and woman living together in a committed relationship. Always she'd met the infant's mother first. Not this time.

"Where's Mrs. Garrett?" she asked.

"I'm not married."

"But Brady has a mom."

He frowned and his perpetual dark look grew positively black. "The woman who gave birth to him is not going to be a part of his life."

Was that his way of saying she'd passed away? If only there'd been time for Ginger to fully brief her on this position.

"Is she—I mean, was there a medical problem?"

"Nothing like that. All you need to know is that she won't be an issue." And the scowl on his face put an end to further questions on the subject.

She had news for him. A mother who disappeared from your life could be an even bigger issue. Maggie knew from firsthand experience.

"Now, if it's all right with you," he continued, "I have a few questions."

"I'm an open book," she said.

"May I see your references?"

"I didn't bring anything with me."

"Then you're the first who's arrived without them."

"I'm between assignments, Mr. Garrett, and was expecting to have several weeks off. Ginger said this was an emergency and I should come right away. She promised to messenger over whatever paperwork was required."

"I require it before you interact with my son."

"Then we have a problem."

She stared at the little boy in her arms who was sucking on his little fist and staring up at her with his father's dark eyes. There was a funny sort of tightness in her chest just before she felt a powerful tug on her heart. He was a beautiful child, but that wasn't a surprise because his father was an incredibly handsome man.

This was a first, too. She normally felt nothing but the

general nurturing instincts that babies always generated in her. This was different. Because there was no mother in the picture? Because she was one of a long line of nannies in his short little life? Because Jason Garrett clearly needed her? Or was it the man himself?

He was as compelling as any Gothic romance hero she'd ever read. He was Mr. Darcy, Heathcliff and Edward Rochester all rolled into one tall, muscular, attractive and dashing package.

She would be the first to admit that her hormones hadn't been out for a test drive in quite a while. But they were making up for lost time in a big way now. This father-son duo packed a powerful punch in the few minutes she'd been here. How much damage could they do if given half a chance? It was a disaster in the making.

"I don't think I can work for you, Mr. Garrett." She shifted the baby into his arms and the way he instantly stiffened told her he wasn't used to this.

She refused to let her sympathy cloud her better judgment and walked out of the room.

"Ms. Shepherd—" He caught up with her in the foyer. "Wait—"

Bracing herself, she turned to face him but could only raise her gaze to the collar of his shirt. "There's no point in wasting any more of your time."

"It's my time and I'm asking for just a few more minutes of yours."

"I don't think there's anything left to say."

"That's where you're wrong."

"I'm wrong?" she said, taking her purse from the table and sliding the strap over her shoulder.

The baby started to whimper and flail his fists and the just-this-side-of-panic look was back in his father's eyes. "Okay. Maybe I've been a little hasty in judgment. But look at it from my perspective."

"And what is that?"

It was a mistake to ask, but that wasn't her first one. Going soft when he all but admitted he was wrong was the number one slip-up.

"Nanny number one couldn't soothe him, and made some excuse about why it's all right to let babies cry during the night. When my son cries it's because he needs tending to and I'm in favor of feeding on demand as opposed to making him wait for a scheduled time."

"I agree." To her way of thinking babies always had a reason for crying and should not be ignored. The child came first. Period. The caretaker was always on call. "What happened to nanny number two?"

"A family emergency." He glanced at his son, a fiercely protective look. "Something I understand all too well."

She'd never had a family, at least not a traditional one. "That's not her fault."

"No, but now it's my problem. And I have to ask—you walked in and had him quiet in thirty seconds flat—how did you do that?"

She shrugged. "I'm good at what I do, Mr. Garrett."

"I couldn't say about babies in general," he said, a smile cutting through his uncompromising expression. The transformation was amazing. "But I saw for myself that with my son you're very skilled."

She wasn't the only one. Her skill was infants, his was flattery. At first he'd kept it securely under wraps, along with his seriously compelling charm. Now that he needed them, he pulled out both and set them on stun. "Brady is a beautiful child."

"He's more than that, Ms. Shepherd—"

"Maggie."

He nodded. "He's my son, Maggie. I'm a demanding boss. I'll admit that. And I don't know a lot about babies. I'll admit that, too. But most important for you to know is that I'm a protective father. It seems to me that when caring for a child there are some basic nonnegotiable principles."

"Such as?"

"Doing your job. When I arrived home from the office unexpectedly, I found nanny number three on the balcony with a glass of wine and Brady in his crib crying."

Maggie was shocked. "That's horrific."

"I thought so, too, and fired her on the spot."

"Good for you."

"So, you see, I find myself in a situation. I have a business to run."

"I've heard of it. Garrett Industries is developing that huge project just off the 15 freeway, the one monopolizing all the construction cranes in the Southwest." When he grinned again, her chest felt funny even before her pulse fluttered.

"There's nothing I'd like better than to stay home and care for my son, but I have obligations. People are counting on me and I'm counting on you. I'm in great need of your services."

"What about my references?"

"I understand that there's no way to measure a person's ability to do a good job, but it would reassure me to see something in writing that says you're qualified to care for children. But I'd like to hire you right now, references pending."

When Brady started to whimper harder, she really felt as if this was a father-son tag team. They were piling it on. His crying went from half-hearted to off the chart in a matter of seconds and Jason handed him back to her.

"Hey, sweetie," she soothed, and tried stroking his palm again. After several heaving sobs he started to quiet.

"I think I've just seen all the references necessary," Jason said. "He wouldn't stop crying for me and I offered him a thousand dollars. The interview is over, you're hired."

Maggie wasn't so sure this was a good idea, but she simply couldn't walk out on this child. "Okay."

* * *

"Brady is asleep."

Jason looked up and saw Maggie in the doorway to his study. He'd been completely focused on the information in the envelope that Ginger Davis had messengered over. Reading about his new nanny was priority number one and he'd forgotten about asking her to join him when the baby was settled.

Sitting behind his flat oak desk in his home office, he held out a hand. "Have a seat."

She picked the left wingchair across from him, then folded her hands in her lap as she met his gaze.

"Is Brady all right?"

"He's an angel," she said, smiling for the first time. "He's bathed, fed and sleeping like a baby."

"Good." He nodded toward the stack of papers. "Ginger is very efficient."

"I've always found her to be a woman of her word."

Good to know because The Nanny Network charged a hefty amount of money for the service provided. Everything in life came with a price tag, but you didn't always know if it would be worth what you paid.

In the case of his son, he wasn't disappointed. He'd never known a love like he'd felt when he saw Brady for the first time. And the feeling had multiplied tenfold since he'd brought him home from the hospital. When Catherine had broken the news about the unplanned pregnancy, her next comment was that *it* would be history soon. Jason couldn't accept that his child would be removed as if it were nothing more than an inconvenience, an annoyance, a stain on the carpet.

After intense negotiation and a large settlement, he had a son whose mother received a bonus for signing off all rights to him. He'd have paid her far more than she'd happily taken, but that had been enough to finance plastic surgery or any other physical enhancement to further her acting ambitions.

What he hadn't counted on was how complicated finding competent child care would be.

"So you finally have my references?" Maggie asked.

Her voice pulled him back from the memories, and he glanced at her before again scanning the résumé that included very thorough background information. "You're an orphan?"

"That would assume my parents are dead. In fact, I don't know where they are. I never knew them at all. As an infant I was left on the steps of the Good Shepherd Home for Children where I was found by Sister Margaret and Sister Mary."

Her tone was so moderate and matter of fact it was several moments before the pieces formed a complete picture. She'd been no bigger than Brady when she was discarded, an annoyance, an inconvenience. "So Margaret Mary Shepherd—"

She nodded. "I was named after two nuns and a home for abandoned children."

It wasn't often that people surprised him, but he was surprised now. "Forgive me, I don't know what to say."

"That implies you pity me."

"No, I—"

"It's all right. I consider myself lucky. Everyone was good to me. No one turned me away when I asked for more gruel." She smiled at her reference to the famous scene in the dark Dickens book. "I had a roof over my head, a bed to sleep in and people who cared about me. I'm healthy and privileged to do a job I love. I didn't end up in a Dumpster or as a sensational, sad headline in the newspaper. It could so easily have been a story with a tragic ending, but someone cared enough to give me to the sisters."

Catherine hadn't cared, but for a price she'd given him Brady.

Maggie Shepherd met his gaze and her own was unapologetic, clear-eyed and proud. There was no sign that he intimidated her and he wasn't sure how he felt about that. Considering his recent nanny problems he'd have preferred a healthy dose of fear.

At first sight he'd thought her plain, although her wide dark-blue eyes that sort of tilted up at the corners were very unusual. Her brown hair was pulled back in a long ponytail. If worn long, it would spill over the shoulders of her turtleneck sweater and down her back. For some reason, he wanted very much to see it loose, maybe so that she'd look older, less like a fourteen-year-old babysitter.

When she'd held his son and smiled, the mouth he'd thought a bit too wide was suddenly intriguing. The tender expression in her eyes when she looked at the baby made her beautiful. Not home-run-with-the-score-tied-in-the-ninth-inning exciting, or touchdown-to-take-the-lead-with-thirty-seconds-left-in-the-fourth-quarter stunning. But the individual features blended on a canvas of pale, flawless skin mixed with an air of sweetness and formed a pretty picture.

He folded his hands and settled them on the desk as he leaned forward. "Do you wonder about your parents?"

Her serene look didn't slip. "It's a waste of energy."

"But aren't you curious about anything?" He couldn't help wondering if Brady would have questions about where his mother was and why she'd disappeared from his life. The truth wasn't pretty, and Jason wasn't prepared to tell it. But at least he knew what the truth was. Maggie had no details about her parents and he wondered if that bothered her. "Do you ever think about where they are? What they're like? Why you are the way you are?"

She stared at him for a moment, then stood, serenity suddenly shattered. "If this is your way of saying you think I'm unsuitable for the nanny position…"

He stood, too, and noticed for the first time how small she was. Fragile, almost. He towered over her and now it made him feel like a bully until he remembered her fierce determination to comfort a distressed baby. She'd been like a force of nature.

"I didn't mean to pry," he said. "But I feel within my

rights as a father to know the woman in whose care I'm leaving my son."

"If you don't trust me, I'd appreciate it if you'd simply say so."

"There's nothing in your background, personal or professional, that made me change my mind about hiring you."

"Fine. Then, if it's all right with you, I'll go settle in while Brady is sleeping."

"Will you stay for another moment? I have just a few more questions."

She hesitated, then sat down again. "All right."

"When did you first become aware that you're a 'baby whisperer'?" he asked, rounding the desk to sit on the corner closest to her. "I'm just curious."

"I've always been around children. Everyone at the home was expected to help out, but it never felt like a chore to me. Then my first job while I worked my way through college was with a wealthy family who had four children, ranging in age from an infant to early twenties. He was in college." Her lips pressed together for a moment before she added, "I found I liked babies."

But she hadn't liked something. Jason wondered about that and also about what she did after college graduation. Her background information had only said that she'd spent time in the convent without taking final vows.

"Why did you decide to become a nun?"

"I admired the sisters and wanted to be like them. It was important to me to give back, help people the way I'd been helped." Her face was all innocence and sincerity that couldn't quite hide the shadows.

"There are many altruistic professions that don't require such a structured lifestyle," he said.

"I knew what I was leaving behind in the secular life."

So she'd dated and still chose to enter the convent. Or maybe dating drove her *into* the convent.

"You didn't find what you were looking for with the nuns?" He was pushing the boundaries of this interview and he knew it. But she stirred his curiosity.

She sighed and thought for several moments before answering, as if choosing her words carefully. "It wasn't a matter of not finding what I was looking for in the convent as much as I'm simply not good nun material."

The corners of his mouth curved up. "Oh?"

"When you're close to final vows, it's a time for reflection and honesty. I simply had too many doubts."

"About what?"

"Me." She shrugged. "There was an expectation of sacrifice and commitment that I wasn't sure of being able to sustain."

"I see," he said.

"And speaking of expectations—" she shifted in her chair, and met his gaze "—it's time we discussed what you expect of me."

"Take care of Brady. He's your only responsibility. I have a cleaning service and a cook who also runs the household. If you need anything let Linda know."

"Fine. But that's not what I meant." She blew out a breath. "It's obvious to me that you're not comfortable with Brady yet. Do you need me to teach you how to take care of him?"

"It's your job to do that."

"I'm not being sarcastic or judgmental," she added quickly. "It's just that this is different for me."

"How so?"

"You're a single father."

"Is that a problem?" he asked, thinking about her first job and the oldest son. Did she get hit on? The thought made him angry. "Like I said before, if I could care for my son, I'd do it in a heartbeat. But I have a large company and need to work."

"I understand. And are the people working for you entitled to scheduled time off?"

"Of course, but—"

"I require one day off a week. Saturday, until midday Sunday. That should be stipulated in the contract that arrived with the rest of the paperwork. Can you handle the baby for a day?" She met his gaze with a direct one of her own and when he hesitated, she said, "Since I've been with The Nanny Network it's never been a problem. But I've never worked in a home where there wasn't a father and a mother."

"Like I said, the woman who gave birth to Brady is a nonissue. I'm paying you to—"

"To be his mother?" she asked.

"No—" He'd paid a woman to bring him into the world and was going to pay Maggie to take care of him. There was no need to put a finer point on it. "Why does this matter?"

"Because you're a single father, it would make good sense for you to find a long-term situation. If I'd known that, I would have turned down the job."

"Why?"

"I only stay for six weeks, then—"

"What?"

"That's also in my contract. My assignments last no longer than that."

Jason didn't want a parade of strangers coming through. He didn't want a revolving door on Brady's care. Continuity and stability were the cornerstones of a well-adjusted childhood and he'd do whatever was necessary to give his son the best cornerstone money could buy. He wanted long term now. He wanted Margaret Mary Shepherd.

She watched him carefully, gauging his reaction. "Ginger will find someone else—"

"What if I don't want someone else?"

From the moment she'd ignored everything but the need to protect a baby—his baby—she'd had him. No one else would do.

Shadows turned her eyes navy blue and she pulled her lips

tight for a moment. "I won't stay beyond what's stipulated in the agreement. It's important that you're aware of that up front."

"Are you already angling for a raise, Maggie?"

"This has nothing to do with money."

Right. And he was Mother Goose.

"Look," he said, rubbing the back of his neck. "This isn't something we need to decide tonight. When the time comes, we'll discuss new terms."

She stood up. "Six weeks, Mr. Garrett."

"Call me Jason."

"All right, Jason. But I'm not budging on my deadline. I won't stay more than six weeks."

He watched the unconsciously sexy sway of her slender hips as she walked out of his office after issuing what could only be construed as a challenge. Obviously Margaret Mary Shepherd had never negotiated with someone who was willing and able to pay whatever it cost to have her.

Chapter Two

Maggie stretched the baby out on her thighs and curled his fingers around her thumbs. "Hey, big boy. Where's that smile? I know you've got one for me," she cooed to him. "Let's see it."

He wasn't five weeks old, and yet he was showing signs that he was on the verge of smiling. Would he look like his father? Her heart tripped up at the thought. This little guy wouldn't be in that heartthrob league yet. The lack of teeth thing could be an issue. But his dad was something else. Jason Garrett had a very nice, very potent smile when he chose to use it. And Brady showed every indication that he'd be the spitting image of his dad.

Stretching out, the baby pressed his little feet into her abdomen and she wondered, not for the first time, what it felt like when life moved inside you. This child was a beautiful miracle, one his mother had walked away from. Not unlike her own mother.

She liked to think lack of money and resources had factored

into the decision to abandon her. But Brady's father clearly had big bucks. The penthouse was understated elegance with recessed lighting, soft yellow paint on the walls, plush white sofas and dark wood tables. Walking on the thick beige carpet was like sinking to your knees in softness. Expertly lighted art hung on the walls and expensive glass pieces and figurines were scattered throughout. In fact, before her tenure here ended, she felt duty bound to remind him to put the pricey stuff up high when Brady got mobile. A toddler's oops in this place could cost way more than most people made in a month.

She glanced out the floor-to-ceiling windows with a spectacular view of the lights on the Las Vegas Strip and the valley beyond. Scenery like that didn't come cheap.

Jason had thoroughly checked her out, and she'd returned the favor, grilling Ginger for information. Her Nanny Network boss had assured her there were no sexual harassment or hostile work environment accusations against him. No hint of scandal or impropriety. Quite the opposite. Everyone who worked for him had only good things to say. Employee retention at his company was exceptionally high.

So why couldn't he retain the mother of his son? Maggie would really like to know the answer to that question.

As if he felt her attention drifting, Brady cooed his irresistible baby coo, and she smiled. "I wasn't ignoring you, sweetie pie. You're a charmer in training, that's what you are."

His mouth curved up at the corners as he happily kicked his feet. She laughed and a corresponding sound gurgled up from deep inside him in what could only have been a laugh.

It was a major "awww" moment, melting her heart like ice on a summer sidewalk. And that was cause for alarm. She didn't do the heart melty thing. That wasn't to say she didn't love babies, all babies. She did. But her thing was not to get attached. On her first day, this little guy had easily hurdled her defenses, then grabbed on to her emotions with both of his tiny hands and the sweetest disposition in the world. He was already starting to feel special and she had enough time left on her commitment for him to do a lot of damage.

Rubbing her thumbs across his tiny knuckles, she smiled. "You are too cute for words, Mr. Garrett."

"Thank you."

The familiar deep voice came from behind her and slid over her senses like warm chocolate and whiskey. Maggie had lost count, but this was the fourth or fifth time today Jason Garrett had dropped in unexpectedly. All that practice should have helped her get used to him. Unfortunately, she wasn't even close to comfortable with Sin City's most eligible bachelor and overachieving tycoon.

"Actually, I wasn't talking to you," she said. "I didn't know you were there. Just like a couple hours ago when you stealthily sneaked up behind me. And the time before that. And the time before—"

"Yeah." He came closer and set his suit jacket on the sofa back, then rested a hip beside it. He leaned forward and smiled at his son. "Hi, buddy," he said, then looked at her. "I get your drift."

"And I get yours."

"I'm not subtle?" he asked.

"Not even a little bit." From the moment they'd met, she'd figured out that he wasn't the most trusting of men. His behavior today was further confirmation. "You're checking up on me."

"Does it bother you?" he asked, not taking the trouble to deny it.

"No. Quite the opposite. I respect you for protecting your son. If every child in the world was cared for so well, it would be a much better place."

What she didn't say was that his defensive actions not only made her respect him, she liked him, too. That was a good thing, right? How come it didn't feel that way? All she felt was uneasy. The last time she'd liked a man this much the feelings had grown into love. He came with a family who liked her back and she'd felt as if she was getting everything she'd always wanted. Then it didn't work out, a major blow that had hurt a lot.

She chanced a glance up at Jason, and her stomach dropped like an airplane hitting turbulence. The sight of him in his rumpled white dress shirt and loosened red tie made it hard to breathe. It was much safer to look at the baby.

"Your daddy's home, Brady. For good this time? Or can we expect ongoing guerrilla warfare tactics this evening?"

"I'm in for the night. You can stand down."

"Good to know."

Jason leaned over again and stirred up the scent of him, something spicy and sexy and all male. Something that made it impossible for her senses to stand down. She felt tingly all over.

He reached out and loosely caught hold of a tiny foot. "Hey, buddy. How are you? Did you have a good day?"

The baby waved his arms and smiled. Jason laughed and the sound warmed her clear through. She was exceptionally good at resisting warm and fuzzy, but there it was again. As if she needed more proof, that double whammy convinced her the combined effect of the Garrett men was pretty potent and highly dangerous stuff. She scooped the baby into her arms, then stood and walked around the sofa.

"He's fed, bathed and in his jammies. All ready to spend some time with his daddy." She settled Brady in his arms and backed away.

This felt weird. After a year at The Nanny Network, Maggie had lots of assignments under her belt. When the man of the house returned from his day at work, Maggie faded discreetly away to give mom and dad couple- and family-bonding time. She waited in the background, ready to jump in and help if needed. The only couple here was father and son. She'd never been in this situation before and didn't quite know what to do with herself.

Jason smiled down at his child. "He smells good."

"Yeah. I don't think anything smells better than a freshly bathed baby."

He looked at her and something dark and dangerous glittered in his eyes for a split second before disappearing. "And he seems pretty happy."

"He's been an angel all day."

"I may be a new father, but I know this mood can disappear in a nanosecond. Before that happens, would you mind taking him while I get out of this suit?"

"Of course."

She took the handoff and tried not to think about him changing. The situation already felt too intimate. She walked around the living room, then into the kitchen. Never in her life had she seen such a beautiful, functional kitchen. Maple cupboards were topped by black granite and in the center was an island big enough for its own zip code. The appliances were stainless steel, including the Sub-Zero refrigerator and two ovens. A glass French door closed off the walk-in pantry that was tidy and organized. In her assignments, Maggie had seen lots of different houses and condos, but never anything as gorgeous as this.

It was past dinnertime and she'd already eaten, but the cook had left a plate for Jason. She felt the need to keep busy and settled Brady in the infant seat on the floor beside the glass-topped dinette. After spinning the toy strung in front of him, she watched him watch it until his interest kicked in. Then she took the plate of lasagna from the fridge, removed the plastic covering and stuck it in the microwave. There was also a salad that she tossed vigorously with Italian dressing.

When Jason returned in his worn jeans and powder-blue

pullover sweater, her insides got a vigorous tossing of their own. He looked as good in casual clothes as he did in slacks and tie. Maybe better, if possible.

She realized she'd been staring and to fill the awkward silence said the first thing that came to mind. "I'm warming up your dinner. You're probably hungry."

"I am." He had a funny sort of intense expression on his face. "If it's all right with you, I'll have a quick bite to eat before hanging out with Brady. Could you stick around?"

"Of course."

He glanced into the microwave. "Something smells good."

"Yeah." And she wasn't at all sure she meant the food. "Linda is a good cook. But you already know that."

"She's been with me for several years."

Stability. Since she never stayed more than six weeks, that was a foreign concept to her. She leaned over the infant carrier and nudged it with a finger, partly to keep nervous hands busy. Partly to rock the baby and stretch out this unpredictable contentment as long as possible.

"I can't help wondering what Linda's job interview was like," she said.

Jason glanced at her over one broad shoulder. "She had terrific references."

"Was there a test? Did she have to prepare pheasant under glass out of corn flakes and tofu?"

He laughed. "Are you implying I'm a demanding boss?"

"Heaven forbid."

"You'd be right. And I won't apologize for it." When the microwave beeped, he retrieved his plate and brought it to the table where his salad waited. "I don't demand more of anyone else than I'm willing to give. That said, working with food is relatively easy. Babies, not so much. Because I'm willing to give everything I've got."

"You're his father. That's the way it should be." She didn't have the right to give everything and had to hold part of herself back. Otherwise, leaving hurt too much.

Brady's snorts and grunts changed tone indicating that the grumpy portion of the evening was about to commence. She was grateful for the distraction because the words made her like Jason even more. "I'll take him into the other room so you can eat in peace."

"Stay." He put a hand on her arm and stared at it for a second before meeting her gaze. Shrugging, he added, "Peace is highly overrated. I haven't seen him all day."

"I beg to differ. What with the unannounced visitations."

"Let me rephrase. I haven't had a chance to spend quality time with him. Keep me company. It won't take long to wolf this down."

Her arm tingled from his touch and she felt strange, out of her element, which made her want to run and hide. But how could she refuse? Especially when he said it like that. Not to mention that he was the boss.

"Okay."

But when she tried to sit, the baby wasn't happy. She stood and her body automatically started a gentle swaying motion. She turned Brady so his back was against her chest and father and son could see each other. She caressed the baby's palm with her thumb because he seemed to like that.

"So, tell me," Jason said, "what did I miss today? What did you do?"

"Let me see," she started. "I changed diapers. Fed this little guy. Played with him. Sang songs—for your information, his favorites are 'Row, Row, Row Your Boat' and 'Rubber Ducky.'"

"He told you that?" Jason chewed as he studied her.

"Not in so many words. But in body language, he was rockin' out."

"Meaning he didn't have a meltdown during the performance?"

"Pretty much," she confirmed.

He laughed, then forked up a bite of salad. After chewing, he asked, "What else?"

She thought about the day. "He took two naps, during which I'm quite sure he had a significant growth spurt. I can feel the difference in density already."

"In one day?"

"Absolutely."

Singing his son's praises and giving the blow-by-blow of Brady's day made her feel more connected than she liked. And protective. She couldn't shake the sensation of wanting to go run interference for him because he was starting out life with one strike against him. Like her.

Jason smiled tenderly at the boy. "Way to go, buddy. Getting bigger is your job."

"Speaking of jobs," Maggie said. "What did you do today?"

Thoughtfully, he chewed a bite of lasagna and washed it down with water. "I had a great day. In between nanny surveillance, I closed a billion-dollar deal, which will net enough money to make a significant donation to a prestigious university. It's more than enough to ensure that my son will be accepted and get into whatever program he wants."

"So you bought him a way into college?"

He tilted his head thoughtfully. "Let's say I removed any doubt."

He was a man who had the means to get what he wanted.

Twenty-four hours ago Jason had said he wanted her, and here she was. The thought set off a powerful quivering in the pit of her stomach as she recalled the dark and determined look on his face when he'd made the pronouncement.

He *wanted* her.

That was a heady notion, a thought she refused to take any further.

After Jason finished eating, he set his dishes in the sink,

then took the baby from her. Murmuring tenderly, he settled Brady in the crook of his muscular arm, and Maggie barely managed to hold in a sigh.

Was there anything more appealing than the sight of a handsome man holding a tiny infant in his strong arms? If so, she'd never seen it.

She watched the two Garrett men walk away, although technically only one was walking. But that didn't change the fact that she was alone. Along with the solitude, common sense came pouring in. She'd never felt a pull on her heart like this. Was it because she was a stand-in mom, being the only female on the premises? Is that why she was feeling so connected to the single father and his motherless baby?

Whatever the reason, she had to stop. She was an employee, a very temporary one, nothing more. Soon she would be a nanny to another baby. And darned if the thought of leaving was about as appealing as a header off the top of the Stratosphere. It must have something to do with the fact that they were a family without a mom and she was a woman without a family.

This strong reaction, with five weeks and six days to go, made her wish she hadn't agreed to stay at all.

Jason wasn't accustomed to concentration problems when he worked—either at the office, or at his home office, which was where he was now. The baby had changed his life in so many ways, and could be a distraction, but that wasn't the problem. It had nothing to do with adjusting to his new situation and everything to do with the new nanny.

Maggie.

Margaret Mary Shepherd wasn't the sort of woman who would normally capture his notice. She wasn't classically beautiful nor did she have legs that went on forever. As a matter of fact, he'd never seen her legs except covered by denim, apparently the uniform of efficient nannies these days. Her appeal was all about character. She was dependable, efficient and sarcastically witty.

Admittedly, his taste in women left a lot to be desired. Case in point: his son's biological mother who had required a large sum of money to guarantee Brady's very existence.

Maggie wasn't like that. If she was, it would have been easier to put her out of his mind.

A soft knock sounded on his study door. It couldn't be Brady, so by process of elimination… His stomach tightened just a fraction with what felt like anticipation.

"Come in," he said.

And there was his distraction in the flesh, wearing jeans and a yellow sweater, looking a lot like a slice of sunshine.

"Maggie. Hi."

"Sorry to interrupt."

"Not a problem." He removed his glasses and turned off the computer, giving her his full attention—full, because she'd already had part of it since she arrived five days ago. "What can I do for you? Is Brady okay?"

"Fine. He was a little fussier than normal tonight. I hope he didn't disturb you."

"Never." Thoughts of her had disturbed him, but that wasn't her problem. Nor was it something he intended to share. "Any idea why he was restless?"

She stayed in the doorway. "Babies are a guessing game. He could have been overtired. Maybe gas. There's no way to know. You listen to the various cries—"

"It all sounds the same to me." Jason leaned back in his chair and linked his fingers over his abdomen. "They're different?"

"Very." She smiled. "There's a frantic edge to it when he's hungry. A sort of general dissatisfaction when he needs to be changed. Kind of a quiet mewling sound when he's telling you off because his need wasn't met in a timely fashion."

"Fascinating." As was the fact that she hadn't moved any closer to his desk. "Where are my manners? Come in and have a seat."

"Oh—I just wanted to remind you—"

He motioned her in and indicated one of the matching wing chairs in front of him. The smooth leather had gold buttons. Very pretentious. Very not her, but what could you do? "Please sit."

"Okay." She started to close the door the way it had been, then hesitated and opened it wide. "I need to listen for the baby."

"Of course." That was her job. She worked for him. At the office he didn't find it necessary to remind himself that any woman was his employee. But it was different with Maggie. Must have something to do with the intimacy of living under the same roof.

She sat in front of him and the movement brought the scent of her wafting to him. It was sweet, which suited her.

"I just wanted to remind you that tomorrow is Saturday—my day off. And I won't be back until noon on Sunday. You'll have to get up with Brady if he needs anything. Should I notify Ginger to send someone to fill in?"

He thought about it for a moment, then shook his head. "I'm looking forward to time with my son."

"Okay."

The smile she gave him was full of approval and he felt like he'd given the correct game-show answer that would make all his dreams come true. Her reaction shouldn't be that important to him.

"Do you have plans for the day?" he asked, mostly to distract himself from the unsettling thought.

"I'm going to do what I do every Saturday."

"And that is?"

"Volunteer at the Good Shepherd Home."

"I see." No shopping? Lunch with the girls? A manicure,

pedicure or facial? He was lying. He didn't see at all. "What
do you do there?"

"I fill in for one of the staff who takes a day off. And to
answer your question, I do whatever needs doing. Cooking.
Cleaning. Playing with the kids. Talking to them. Tucking
them in at night. It's important they know people care, that
they're not leftovers. Throwaways."

"Is that how you felt?"

The question came out before he could stop it. His only
excuse was that part of his mind was focused on her mouth,
and its high sexiness factor. If she wasn't his son's nanny,
he'd kiss her, take those unusually tempting lips out for a
spin and see if they tasted as good as they looked. But she
was the nanny and it wouldn't be smart. He couldn't think
about himself when Brady needed her. And his son's needs
came first.

He shook his head. "Forgive me for prying. That's really
none of my business."

"It's all right." She sighed. "Probably wouldn't be normal
for me not to have abandonment issues. Not letting that define
your life is the challenge. My goal is to help the kids understand that message."

"You're a good person."

She shrugged and her gaze lowered to the hands clasped
in her lap. "I'm just trying to give back."

"The home's gain is my loss," he said. Standing, he
rounded the desk and rested one hip on the corner, just an
arm's length from her. He wouldn't kiss her, but he wanted to
get closer. Out of the frying pan into the fire. "Traditionally
Saturday is date night. Your benevolence will put a speed
bump in my social life."

"Speed bump?" She met his gaze and spirit sparkled in her
eyes. "You probably beat the women back with a stick."

"Not lately." He laughed. "Now that I think about it, dating is tedious. Time consuming. Hectic and energy draining. Especially now when I need all the energy I have for Brady."

Again she gave him the approving smile. "Then you should think about settling down. Getting married. Did you know studies have shown that married men live longer?"

"I hadn't heard that."

"Oh, I know marriage takes energy." The earnest expression on her face was cute and incredibly appealing. "But a committed relationship is different. And the rewards make it worth the effort."

Not in his opinion. "And how do you know this? Have you been married?"

"Me?" She touched a hand to her chest. "No. But I've observed a lot of happy, contented couples who are united in their dedication to raising a family and making a life together."

"You get around."

She lifted her shoulders in a shrug. "Occupational hazard."

A subtle reminder that her time with him was finite. She didn't know it yet, but she wouldn't have to look for another job.

"From my perspective, marriage provides nothing but stress and discord," he said.

"Really?"

"Oh, yeah." *And then some,* he thought. "It doesn't work and inevitably leads to divorce and disillusionment or the demise of dreams. At the very least it causes bitterness and resentment."

She frowned. "May I ask what your perspective is?"

"My father. He's currently involved in financial negotiations in a divorce from wife number four and engaged to number five. I've had a front-row seat to discord and dying dreams."

The look she gave him was filled with pity. "I'm sorry."

"Don't be." His tone was more sharp than he'd intended. "It was and continues to be a good education. It's cost Dad a lot of money, a good portion of which goes to the army of accountants he employs to keep up with alimony payments."

"For what it's worth," she said, "I can see where that would give you pause. I might have abandonment issues, but at least I had stability. The nuns at Good Shepherd gave me that."

He didn't plan to debate the benefits and drawbacks of growing up in an orphanage versus the marriage-go-round of his own childhood. He had a thing about commitment; she had abandonment issues. That was information he would tuck away for another time.

He folded his arms over his chest. "Now that I'm a father, I can see where a case could be made for constancy. I'd be lying if I said it—marriage—hadn't crossed my mind."

"That's the spirit," she said.

He held up his hands. "Whoa. Finding someone to marry is a nice fantasy, but it's easier said than done."

"Are you one of those men who manufactures flaws in every woman he meets?"

"That's a loaded question."

"And probably none of my business. But you started it." She tilted her head to the side and her silky ponytail brushed the shoulder of her sweater making his fingers itch to do the same. "I just meant that some men find the smallest excuses to walk away from a relationship, not really trying to make it work."

"And you know this from firsthand experience?" Since he'd started the prying, what was the harm in a little more?

"Magazines. Articles in women's periodicals."

None of that was helpful information. "You don't date?"

"I have two problems with dating."

"Only two?" he asked.

She laughed. "Number one is lack of time. Between my job and working at the home, there's very little left over."

"What's number two?"

"Lack of men."

"Excuse me?"

"Think about it. My day revolves around infants. I go from job to job. It's pretty intense." She gave him a wry look. "And energy consuming. Besides, where am I going to meet someone?"

It was on the tip of his tongue to ask if he was chopped liver, but he figured that wasn't a place he was prepared to go for too many reasons to list. But right at the top was the fact that he was way too pleased she didn't meet men.

And suddenly the temptation to touch her was too much to resist when he was this close. And he didn't trust himself to only touch her. Straightening, he moved back around to the other side of his desk, putting distance between them.

"I'm the last person who should give you advice," he said.

"Actually, I think Sister Margaret and Sister Mary are the last ones to give advice on the dos and don'ts of dating."

He couldn't stop the grin. Wicked, witty sarcasm. It was incredibly intriguing. "Okay. Point taken."

She looked thoughtful. "For what it's worth, the most advantageous environment for Brady is one with positive male and female role models. That said, when you meet the right woman, you should snap her up."

"That's a challenge to do without Saturday nights. And make no mistake, it will take a lot of dating to get it right."

"I'm sorry I won't be around to watch."

"I should think your curiosity would be powerful motivation to stay," he said.

"There's only five weeks left on my contract and I can't extend it." Genuine regret darkened her eyes.

And she wasn't the only one. Unlike the other nannies he'd had, he actually liked Maggie. She was direct and didn't play games. On top of that she was incredibly good with his son. He couldn't imagine her being more loving, tender and nurturing if she'd actually given birth to the boy. In the nanny department, this time was indeed the charm. Did she really think he would let her get away without a fight?

Not so fast, Margaret Mary Shepherd. She hadn't seen his very best stuff yet.

Chapter Three

"Good job on the bedtime prayers, Lyssa." Maggie pulled the sheet and blanket up, then leaned over and kissed the six-year-old's cheek.

In this wing of the home, the little girl was the youngest and the last of her ten charges to be tucked in. There were fifty children, from birth to eighteen, being cared for here and Maggie relieved one of the paid employees who took a much-needed day off. Her commitment to Good Shepherd Home for Children was unwavering because without this place, she wasn't sure what would have become of her. The nuns continued to protect and care for kids who desperately needed them and Maggie considered it a sacred honor to assist in any way she could.

"Maggie?"

She felt a small hand patting her arm and looked at the blue-eyed, blond cherub clutching a tattered blanket. "What is it, sweetie?"

"I asked God to bring my mommy back."

If Maggie had a dollar for every child who'd said that, she'd be a wealthy woman. The words never failed to tug at her heart because she knew exactly how the little girl felt. "I'm sure God will do His best to answer your prayer."

Lyssa rubbed a finger beneath her nose. "But I thought God can do anything."

She always hated this part. The children received religious instruction and were taught that the Lord is all powerful and merciful. The kids eventually came up with the same questions she had. If God loves me and takes care of me, then why don't I have a mom or dad? In Lyssa's case, her drugged-out mother and a boyfriend had abandoned the little girl at the bus station. There was no way this child would understand that God *had* taken care of her by making sure she was with the nuns here at Good Shepherd.

"God can do anything, sweetie."

"Why did He let her go away?"

She met the child's innocent gaze and wondered how to explain when she didn't understand it herself. "All I can tell you is that God always does things right, even if it seems wrong to us."

"Is it okay that I asked Him to bring Mommy back?"

"Of course." Maggie stroked the hair away from the small face. "Just remember that if you ask Him for something and you don't get it, you have to trust."

"Why?"

"Because you can be sure He'll give you what you need at the appropriate time. God can do anything He thinks is best."

"I think my mommy is best."

Maggie managed to smile even though the words hurt her heart. "And I think you're pretty special."

"I love you, Maggie."

"I love you, too, sweetheart."

When the little girl yawned and rolled to her side, Maggie let out a sigh of relief. For now she'd dodged the issue with Lyssa. But she couldn't help thinking about the infant in the luxurious penthouse in the center of Las Vegas who would one day be asking his father a similar version of the question: Why isn't my mother here with me? Why didn't she love me enough to stay? In Maggie's case, eventually the questions had hollowed out a place inside that became a need for someone to love her, someone who didn't have to because it was their job. Someone to love her just for herself. Now she channeled that need into the extra-special care she gave every child who came into her life.

After one final glance at the four other twin beds in the room, she was satisfied that everyone was sleeping soundly. She turned on the nightlight and left the door open in order to hear the children during the night.

The house was a big Victorian located on Water Street in the Old Henderson section. Rumor had it that there'd been a brothel here once upon a time. Then the church acquired the property and turned it into a children's home.

Maggie had spent a good portion of her life here and thought how different this place was from Jason's posh penthouse. At the bottom of the wooden stairs there was a living room on her right and dining room on the left. Neither functioned in that capacity. Worn furniture and toy boxes said loud and clear that this was a place for children.

Her steps echoed on the wooden floor as she headed to the kitchen in the back of the house. Cold in body and spirit, she thought a cup of coffee would hit the spot. When she entered the large room with rows of tables and benches, she saw Sister Margaret sitting by herself, deep in thought.

Maggie loved this woman—not just *like* a mother. Sister Margaret Connelly was the only mother she'd ever known. And she looked troubled.

"They're asleep," she said, moving farther into the room.

Sister looked up and smiled. "Thank you, Maggie."

"I was just going to pour myself a cup of coffee. Can I get one for you?"

"That would be nice, dear. I just made a pot."

Maggie knew that because Sister always made a pot for their catching-up chat, a cherished weekly ritual. She smiled as she walked over to the old white stove with the electric coffeemaker beside it. She reached up and opened the battered-oak cupboard door and pulled out a green mug for herself and a blue one for Sister. After pouring the steaming liquid and putting sugar and cream in each, she carried both to the long, picniclike table and sat down across from the nun.

Maggie wrapped her hands around the warm mug, which felt incredibly good on a cold January night, and studied the woman who'd raised her. The order she belonged to didn't wear habits and veils. That clothing was too restrictive for their active work with the children. She was in her usual uniform of striped cotton blouse, black slacks and thick, co-ordinating sweater. Blue-eyed, brown-haired Sister Margaret was in her early fifties with the spirit of a much younger woman. But tonight the years were showing and it had nothing to do with the silver strands in her hair.

"Is something wrong, Sister?"

"I was just savoring the quiet. It's such a rare occurrence in a house with so many children."

"You can say that again." There were times at Jason's, when Brady was sleeping soundly, that she experienced the quiet and missed the rowdy sounds of the kids. Loud and lively were normal to her.

"You must be tired, dear. That art project with the younger children must have worn you out. I can't believe you were up for using real paint."

Maggie nodded. "It was a little hectic. But the kids loved

it. And keeping them busy is the goal." On Saturday there was no school so channeling the energy was an ongoing challenge for her and the other volunteers.

"Speaking of keeping busy, didn't you just take on a new job?" Sister blew on her steaming mug. "Where are you working?"

"Spring Mountain Towers."

The nun's eyebrows rose. "That's some pricey property."

"No kidding. In the penthouse, no less. The infant is completely adorable. His name is Brady Garrett."

The nun took a sip of her coffee and studied Maggie over the rim. "And something's troubling you. What is it, dear?"

"I can't stop worrying about him when I'm not there."

"You've been coming to Good Shepherd on Saturday since you started working as a nanny and this is the first time you've ever expressed concern about the child in your care."

"This is the first time I've left the infant with a father and no mother."

"Where is his wife?"

"He doesn't have one." Maggie remembered him talking about dating and her vision of him with lots of women. The idea was oddly disturbing to her. "Jason—he's Jason Garrett—"

"The billionaire developer?"

"The very one. He only said that the baby's mother won't be an issue."

"If only," Sister said.

"Amen." Lyssa's bedtime prayer for God to bring her mother back still echoed in Maggie's heart. Jason had more money than he would ever need and couldn't give his son the one thing every child wanted most.

"What's he like?" Sister asked.

How did she describe Jason Garrett? Her pulse fluttered and skipped just thinking about him. "He's driven. Focused. He loves his son very much."

"You left out seriously cute," Sister added, blue eyes twinkling.

"I beg your pardon?" Maggie pretended to be shocked.

"I've seen his picture in the paper. And he was in that magazine's yearly issue of best-looking bachelors." Sister grinned. "I'm a nun, not dead."

"Clearly." Maggie laughed. "You're right. He's seriously cute—even better looking in person."

"So if he's devoted to his son, why are you worried about the baby?"

"What if Brady is upset and Jason can't quiet him? I showed him the five S's—" Sister slid her a blank look and she added, "The five S's of soothing a baby. I've taught the technique to the volunteers here who work with infants. It was developed by Dr. Harvey Karp at UCLA. Swaddling, side lying, swinging, shushing and sucking. You wrap him tightly in a receiving blanket to simulate the security of the womb, hold them on their side in your arms, swing gently back and forth and make a shushing noise."

"That seems simple enough."

"Maybe." She caught her bottom lip between her teeth. "But Jason builds big resorts. He's not a baby kind of guy. What if he can't handle it? What if he—"

"Needs you?"

"I know that sounds arrogant—"

Sister reached over and squeezed her hand. "Not at all, Maggie. It just shows how much you care. And I worry you'll get hurt because of that marshmallow heart of yours. You have to be careful."

The warning was too late, but Sister didn't know about that. Now there was no point in making both of them feel bad. "I'm a big girl now."

"That doesn't mean I don't still worry about you." Sister shook her head. "Some children never get over a deep anger and resentment about growing up in an orphanage, present company excepted. You were always a sweet child, loving easily and accepting without question."

That may have been true when she lived here, but that changed after she fell in love and then lost even more than her heart. She still cared deeply, especially about children, but now she had parameters in place for her own protection. That way she didn't have to hold part of herself back. But she was already more attached to Brady than she'd ever been to an infant and it had only been a week. That didn't bode well for her marshmallow heart.

"I'm older and wiser now, Sister."

"That sounds ominous."

"I just meant that as a working woman of the world I've acquired experience."

"You sound sad."

"No." Maggie shrugged. "I guess all the constant moving around in my job is making me restless. Making me yearn for stability."

Odd. It hadn't occurred to her when they talked, but that was something she and Jason had in common.

Sister's eyes filled with sympathy. "I didn't know you felt that way."

Maggie hadn't, until very recently.

"It's just that I haven't felt like I belonged since I left here at eighteen. When I entered the convent after college—" She ran her index finger around the rim of her mug. "I think I was looking for roots, like I had here at the home." Maggie saw the worry she'd noticed earlier in the nun's expression. "What is it, Sister?"

"It's not your problem—"

"So there is something."

Sister sighed. "The state has scheduled an inspection of this building."

"Isn't that standard procedure?"

"Yes. But we've been aware for some time that the home needs extensive and expensive repairs—starting with a roof and the plumbing and it's not in our operating budget. The diocese doesn't have the money, either." She shook her head. "We're hoping to get by just one more time, but if we don't, they could shut us down."

"But where will the children go?" Maggie couldn't imagine what would have happened to her without the love and support of Sister Margaret and everyone else here at Good Shepherd.

"We're looking into alternative placements, but the state is already burdened with more children than they can care for."

"Is there anything I can do to help?" Maggie asked.

Sister tried to smile. "That's very sweet of you, dear. But I don't think so. The Lord provides, and every day I ask Him to provide for us."

Maggie would pray, too. For Lyssa's sake, and all the rest of the kids at Good Shepherd, she hoped the volume of prayers would produce a miracle.

In his study, Jason looked at the computer screen to check his e-mail and rubbed his hands over his face, scraping his palms on the scruff of beard he hadn't had time to shave. He was bone tired. If he didn't know better, he'd swear a gravel truck had overturned in his eyes. Brady had been up every two hours during the night. The only way he'd napped was while being held and rocked. Jason had always thought building a resort was stressful, but that was before becoming a father. Right now he'd welcome budget woes, a spike in the cost of building materials and labor disputes.

And Maggie.

He'd take her in a heartbeat. As if his son heard that thought, the baby let out a cry. Just one. Just enough to say he'd need something soon.

"Brady," he groaned, rubbing his hands over his face again. There'd barely been time for a shower, let alone a shave. He looked at the gold clock on his desk. Thirty minutes until noon, when she was due back. If there was a God in heaven she was the punctual type.

He was walking past the foyer on his way to the nursery when the key sounded in the lock just before Maggie walked in. She was better than punctual; she was early.

"Hi," he said, casually lifting a hand in greeting.

"Hi. I'll check on Brady."

"Do you have X-ray hearing?"

"No. Why?" she asked, hurrying down the hall.

"You just opened the door." The baby had been quiet since that one dissatisfied cry. "How did you know he needed something?"

"Whether he did or not, I would have looked in on him. It has nothing to do with super hearing."

"I'm not so sure." He followed Maggie to her room where she set overnight bag on the floor and her purse on the bed. Then she went next door to the nursery. "It's like you're tuned in to his frequency."

"Hi, sweetheart." She lifted the baby out of the crib and cuddled him close. "I missed you."

"I bet you say that to all the boys."

Jason leaned a shoulder in the doorway and folded his arms over his chest as he looked at her. He'd expected a tart comeback to his comment, but there was only silence, which seemed out of character. What the heck did he know about what was or was not in character for a woman who'd come close to being a nun? He'd only known her a week. Still, she seemed like the spunky type and not inclined to overlook an opportunity for a retort.

He'd spent a lot of time in this room over the last few weeks, more than the entire eighteen months he'd lived here.

But he hadn't taken the time to notice what a good job the decorator he'd hired had done. The walls were a pale olive green with white baseboards, crown molding and doors. A changing table in maple stood on one wall with the matching crib beside it. The sheet, quilt and airplane mobile were in shades of green, yellow and pale blue. Stuffed animals filled every flat space and corner of the room. Satisfaction trickled through him that he could give his boy the best.

Including the best of care. Which was all about Maggie.

She kissed Brady's cheek and rubbed his back as her body went into the automatic swaying motion. In her worn jeans, sneakers and pullover red sweatshirt with the words *Good Shepherd* on the front, she was a sight for sore eyes. Weird that the gravel in them was gone now. And he felt as if he was seeing clearly for the first time in over twenty-four hours.

He'd felt her absence, and not because it had been too quiet without her. Brady had filled a lot of the silence with his outstanding pair of lungs. Now that she was here, he had a bad feeling that the deficiency he'd felt had nothing to do with taking care of the baby and that was unsettling.

"How was your day off?" he asked.

"I think he's hungry." She set Brady on the changing table. "When did he last have a bottle?"

Jason glanced at his watch. "About three hours ago."

"Just as I suspected. You're ready to eat." She undid his ter- rycloth sleeper and slid his legs out, grabbing one tiny foot and kissing the toes. "You have hollow legs, Brady Garrett. Yes, you do."

Jason was completely caught up in the tenderness that she lavished on the baby. And apparently he wasn't the only one. When she smiled down, Brady's tiny mouth curved up in response. His arms waved and legs kicked with genuine ex- citement rather than agitation. If that was anything to judge by, the little guy had missed her, too. No, not *too*. That would mean Jason had missed her and he refused to admit to anything but feeling her absence.

He was so caught up in that thought and watching her with his son, it took him several moments to realize she hadn't answered his question about her day off.

Now that he thought about it, she looked tired. There were circles beneath her eyes that made them look even bigger and more vulnerable.

"I'll get a bottle," he said.

"Thanks." She glanced at him for a moment, then finished changing the diaper.

Jason went to the kitchen and took from the fridge one of the formula-filled bottles she'd prepared before leaving yesterday and set it in the automatic warmer. When it was ready, he returned to the nursery where she sat in the glider with Brady.

"Did you have a good time with Daddy?" she said to the baby, holding him close.

As if talking back, the baby made a cooing sound that was new and Jason's chest tightened with tenderness. He'd never worked as hard in his life as he had taking care of his child. His only goal had been to make sure Brady was comfortable, happy and content. But it was nice just to be a spectator and watch, noting the milestones in his son that he'd been too busy to notice.

Maggie smiled at the cooing, and said, "I know, sweetheart. I bet you were an angel. Because you're just the best baby in the whole world. I'm so glad you have food and a place to sleep and a roof over your head."

Her eyes darkened and there was an edge to her voice. For the second time he remembered that she hadn't answered his question. "How was your day off, Maggie?"

She glanced up and held out her hand for the bottle. "See what Daddy brought, Brady?"

He handed it to her, then leaned a shoulder against the wall and watched while the boy latched on to the nipple and eagerly started to suck. Maggie smiled gently but it never chased the shadows from her eyes.

"What's wrong, Maggie?"

Her gaze lifted to his. "Excuse me?"

"How was your day off?"

"Same as always," she said. "I helped with the kids."

He didn't know if her reaction was the same because he had no basis for comparison. No one would accuse him of being the most observant guy on the planet, but even he could see that there was something eating her. "Are you always bothered after spending your day off there?"

"I'm not in the habit of discussing things with my employer."

"Look, I'm a businessman." He slid his fingers into the pockets of his jeans. "And the nature of your employment makes it necessary for you to live under my roof. The lines blur. As your friend *and* employer I ask again, what's wrong?"

She sighed as she set the bottle on the table beside her, then lifted the baby to her shoulder to gently rub his back. Within moments he burped, a sound that did a father proud. Instantly, he started squirming and whimpering, a sign he wasn't finished eating.

When she had Brady settled, Maggie looked up. "What's bothering me? Roofs."

"Would you care to elaborate?"

"Very soon the kids at Good Shepherd may not have one." She sighed. "Sister Margaret told me that the building needs repairs. If they're not done, the state could withhold or refuse to renew a certificate of occupancy, putting their license to operate in jeopardy."

"I see."

Her expression was ironic. "How could you possibly understand? You live in a castle in the clouds. That world is so far removed from your frame of reference."

He couldn't argue with that and decided not to try. "What are they going to do?"

"Sister says they're hoping for an extension that will give them time to come up with a plan. She's been there for a long time and if anyone can come up with a miracle, it's her." She glanced down at the baby who was limp and relaxed in her arms. "She told me not to worry."

"And it's obvious you're following that order."

"Trying to."

Maggie stood with Brady in her arms and looked around the room. "Where's the infant seat?"

"The other room."

She walked out of the nursery, down the hall and stopped dead in her tracks as she surveyed the living room. Jason had been so caught up in having her back that he'd forgotten this chaos. There were blankets, clothes, stuffed animals and toys everywhere. The infant swing, with a onesy hanging from it, stood in front of the sliding doors to the penthouse patio. It seemed a clash of cultures with the landmarks of Vegas just outside.

Numerous used baby bottles sat on the coffee and end tables as if Brady had invited over all his infant buddies and they'd had a blow-out party the night before.

Maggie looked up at him, then back at the clutter and chaos. "So, how did it go?"

"Good." The casual tone was forced. After glancing at the disorder he met her gaze and smiled. "Everything went fine."

"I can't believe you'd stand there and lie to my face when it looks like a gigantic baby store exploded in here."

"It's the truth," he protested. "By my definition of the word fine, that's how it went."

"Oh?"

"Yes. There are no casualties to report. Therefore things went fine."

"Has the cleaning staff seen this place yet?"

He shook his head. "They have the weekend off."

"Well, it won't be fine when they do damage assessment." The corners of her mouth turned up. The spunky comebacks she was firing off were more like the Maggie he knew.

As he watched her easily put the baby in the swing that he'd needed blueprints and specifications to operate, he breathed a sigh of relief. Now that she was back, all was right with his world.

"Maggie?"

She stood and put a finger to her lips as she walked over to him and drew him far enough away to not disturb the baby. "What?"

"Brady missed you."

"He told you that?" she asked, her mouth curving up in a smile.

"Pretty much."

Now that he was this close, he couldn't seem to stop staring at her mouth. "And I'm so glad you're back I could kiss you."

"Always nice to be appreciated."

It was more than that. But he ignored the pull of attraction and concentrated on what was best for Brady and, by extension, himself. After twenty-four hours without her, he never wanted the penthouse to be a Maggie-free zone.

The time had come to step up his campaign to change the terms of her employment.

Chapter Four

Maggie's large, comfortable room in the Garrett penthouse was more like what she imagined a luxury hotel suite would look like, including its own bath. The walk-in closet was big enough to live in and the oak dresser, armoire, headboard and nightstands all matched. No garage sale or flea market stuff here. Brass lamps stood on either side of the king-size bed, which was covered in a beautiful Laura Ashley floral-print comforter. Accent pillows in shades of light pink and rose were piled high. A flat-screen TV was mounted on the wall in the sitting area complete with sofa, recliner and reading lamps.

Hands down, it was the most beautiful space she'd ever had in her life. But all of it paled in comparison to what she'd found on the dresser after settling Brady for the night.

She stared at the black-velvet jewelry box. It was not a very large box and she'd heard that good things come in small packages. Another in a list of gifts from Jason.

For the last four weeks he'd been doing thoughtful things

like this. Flowers. Candy. A generous bonus in her paycheck. All of that was wonderful, but didn't make her heart pound like it was now. She'd have to be deaf, dumb and blind not to know he was wooing her. Not in a romantic way. More of a loyalty retention, boss-employee appreciation sort of way.

But romantic things came in small packages, too. Hand shaking, she reached out and picked it up. In her whole life no one had ever offered her a small black-velvet jewelry box. She'd dreamed and fantasized about Jeff giving her an engagement ring—something that would fit in an elegant container like this. She hadn't thought it could, but her heart pounded even harder.

Even as she ran her index finger over the soft, curved lid, she had an uneasy feeling. Flowers were a sweet gesture. Candy was candy. And a bonus for exemplary work was not out of the ordinary. But this was… She wasn't sure what it was.

"Open it, you nit," she chided herself. Lifting the lid, she gasped when two large diamond-stud earrings winked and sparkled. "Oh, my—"

They were quite possibly the most beautiful things she'd ever seen. And she had to give them back. Right away. Before the idea of trying them on took hold.

If Jason's routine held true to form, this time of night with his son settled in sleep, he could be found working in his study. The door was ajar, with light trickling onto the plush hall carpet. She raised her hand to knock and took a deep breath before tapping lightly.

"Come in."

She pushed the door wide and met his gaze. "May I speak with you?"

"Of course," he said, pushing his glasses to the top of his head.

He'd changed out of his suit into jeans and a white cotton shirt, with sleeves rolled to just above his wrists. The missing power tie did nothing to diminish his power and one look tied her insides up in knots. That was so not how she wanted to feel for this conversation.

She walked in and set the jeweler's box on his desk. "I spent time in the convent, but that doesn't mean I'm stupid and naive."

He glanced down, then met her gaze. "I'm not sure what I did to make you believe I think that, but nothing could be further from the truth."

"You're trying to bribe me into changing my mind about staying as Brady's nanny."

"Bribe isn't an especially flattering word." He closed his laptop. "I prefer the word incentive."

She put her hands on her hips and lifted her chin toward the velvet box. "So you don't deny that's a shameless attempt to convince me to extend my contract?"

"No."

That took the wind out of her sails. "Oh."

"It was the latest in a string of attempts—flowers, candy and a very generous bonus." One dark eyebrow lifted. "All of which you accepted graciously."

"This is different."

"How so?"

Good question. It was personal? Not personal enough? "It just is," she said stubbornly. "I can't accept diamonds. It feels wrong."

"What if I told you they're cheap imitations?"

"Are they?"

"No."

"Then it's too expensive, extravagant and any other *ex* word you can think of," she said.

"Not for me." He smiled, but there was no warmth in it.

"Look, Jason, don't think I'm not grateful that you appreciate my work with Brady—"

"It doesn't look like work when you're with him."

Doesn't feel like it, either, she thought. No way would she tell him that and have him use it against her. "He's a sweet-heart. But I can't stay any longer."

"Why?" There was an angry edge to his voice. "Look, Maggie, I'm not hitting on you."

"I didn't think that." Not really, even though a tiny part of her had hoped.

"Are you afraid I will if you stay? Did someone do that to you?"

"No." If only it had been that ugly. Self-righteous anger would have helped her get over her hurt.

"Then tell me why I can't alter the terms of this agreement and hire you permanently at an incredibly generous salary."

"Because money isn't everything. It doesn't buy happiness."

"It buys a hell of a lot of security."

"It doesn't buy an insurance policy against heartbreak."

"What are you talking about?"

The dark, angry expression on his face chipped away her resolve that her past was no one else's business. Maybe she did owe him an explanation.

She gripped the back of the chair in front of his desk until her knuckles turned white. "When I turned eighteen, I had to leave Good Shepherd because I aged out of the system."

"Aged out?"

"Too old for state funding."

"That stinks."

"Yeah," she agreed. "Fortunately I'd graduated from high school and I was determined to go to college. I had some scholarship money but still needed to work. My experience helping at the home came in handy. I got my first nanny job, which included room and board. I lived with a family and took care of the three minor children."

"Minors? That implies there was an adult child as well."

"The oldest son—Jeff Warren— This is the family I told you about." A vision of brown hair and blue eyes flashed through her mind. He was handsome, smart and sweet. And he broke her heart. "He had a bachelor's degree and was working on his master's."

"And he hit on you?"

"It wasn't like that. We dated."

"And then he hit on you?"

"You have to let that go."

She almost smiled at his tenacity. If she had any stars left in her eyes, she might believe Jason was jealous. But Jeff had taken all the twinkle out of her and left the hard reality in its place.

"What then?"

"We dated. The family liked me and approved of the relationship. We were engaged to be engaged."

"So it was all good?"

"Until Jeff's father got a promotion and was offered the opportunity to build a mega resort in Macau."

He frowned. "I guess he didn't want to commute?"

"No." She laughed and tried to keep the bitterness out of it, although without complete success. "Jeff's parents decided to move the family and gave him the option of finishing school here. He agonized over what to do, but eventually came to the conclusion that a classroom was no substitute for life experience. He moved with the family and we agreed that calls and e-mails would keep us connected. His parents said I was like a daughter to them and promised to keep in touch, too. It wasn't ideal, but we'd formed a bond and I finally had a family."

"But no happy ending?" He removed his glasses from the top of his head and tossed them on the desk. "Otherwise this wouldn't feel like a cautionary tale."

She didn't bother with a short affirmative answer. "He communicated at first, but it lessened over time and finally just stopped. When I called, he admitted that he'd met someone and was engaged."

"Son of a…"

Sadness welled up in her. It wasn't as acute, but still had the power to wound. "His parents eventually stopped communication, which was only natural under the circumstances. But natural didn't make it any easier to come to terms with. I gave them my loyalty, my heart, and I lost everything."

"That's a tough break, Maggie, but—"

"Don't tell me it will be different here. You have to do what's best for your family, and I'm not part of it."

"You're what's best for this family," he said.

"For now. But what if that changes? And don't tell me it won't. I know better." She rounded the chair and sat, gazing intently at him. "After I left the convent, Ginger placed me with a couple who'd just had a baby. Mom was on maternity leave and I helped out, staying on when she returned to work. That baby had me from day one and I gave everything I had because they said the situation was permanent. With my help she could have it all—a career and a baby."

"Don't tell me," he said. "No happy ending here, either."

"After six months she said it was too hard to be away from her child. She was missing too much and wanted to be a stay-at-home mom. So I lost everything again." It shamed her that the memory still brought tears to her eyes. "How could I even be mad? Having a mom is the ideal situation."

A hard look darkened his eyes. "Not if Mom didn't want you in the first place. Not if your own mother doesn't care enough to stick around."

"Is that personal experience talking?"

He shrugged, which neither confirmed nor denied, yet the expression on his face was anything but neutral. It made her curious about him and that was dangerous, another in a long list of reasons why she was right to stick to her time limit.

"It may not seem like a big deal to you, but I never want to go through that again. I've found that my time limit works for me. And Ginger has structured a marketing campaign around my skills and restrictions. I'm an expert at assisting inexperienced parents through the transition and adjustment of a new baby."

"What about my situation?" he asked angrily.

"Ginger has an impressive employee list. Many of them prefer long-term assignments—"

"That's not good enough." He ran his fingers through his hair. "I'm sorry you got hurt in the past. That happens when you wear your heart on your sleeve."

"Not anymore," she protested.

"That's where you're wrong. You still care. Maybe too much, but you can't help that. It's one of your most impressive qualifications. But now your caring has a short shelf life to keep you from getting hurt."

"I'm glad you understand." She stood. "I have a week left on my contract and then I'm leaving."

He stood, too, and towered over her. "Fair warning, Maggie. I'll find a way. Everyone has their price. If you put enough zeros on a check, it takes the sting out of life. However you want to say it, anyone can be convinced."

At the door, she chanced a look at him and felt a pull on her heart. "Not me."

Not with money. However, if he showed the slightest interest in her she wasn't sure the bravado would hold up. She'd walked into his office looking for a fight. Now she realized the reaction was out of proportion to his generous gesture. It was earrings. Big, expensive diamond earrings, but impersonal jewelry nonetheless.

The only reason she could come up with for her meltdown was that she'd half expected to see a ring in the black velvet box. It was stupid and naive, both of which she'd denied being, but that didn't change the truth.

She'd felt the sting of rejection once before, when she learned of Jeff's engagement. When she'd seen the earrings, it was even worse. She'd felt a lot like a mistress who was being appeased. And she'd been disappointed.

This was a sign as big as any on the Las Vegas Strip that she would be lucky if another week here with Jason Garrett didn't cost her as much, or more, than she'd lost in the past.

Maggie had finished packing her clean clothes and had the dirty ones in a laundry bag stashed by the half-opened door. On the tufted-silk bench at the foot of the bed she'd put out a pair of jeans and sweater for when she left in the morning. Ginger had a replacement coming. Jason had met and approved her, however ill-tempered and reluctant his attitude.

Now all she had to do was say goodbye to father and son.

Tears burned the backs of her eyes and her heart squeezed painfully at the thought of leaving. She caught her blurred reflection in the mirror over the dresser. It was going to hurt terribly when she walked out the door for the last time. A sob caught in her throat just before she heard a soft knock on her door.

Jason pushed it wide and stood there. With his tie loosened and the white shirt wrinkled from a long day at the office, he was incredibly appealing. For the last six weeks, it had grown increasingly difficult to keep from saying, "Hi, honey, how was your day?"

Quickly she turned her back to him, hiding the powerful reaction. Oh, God, not now. It was so not the time for her resolve to weaken. Leaving was the right thing for her.

"I'm sorry," she said, struggling to keep her voice steady. "Brady's already asleep. He was just worn out."

"It's all right. I wanted to talk to you anyway."

Too much to hope he wouldn't make one last push to change her mind. A man like him wouldn't be as successful as he was without a dynamic personality, a stubborn streak as wide as the Grand Canyon. Probably it worked for him with women, too. And she might even have changed her mind if her acute response to him just now hadn't convinced her she'd be safer away from him and Brady.

The thought of that sweet little boy punched a hole in the dam of her feelings and the tears she'd barely managed to hold back trickled out.

"There's nothing left to say, Jason." This time her voice broke.

"Are you crying?" He moved close and put his hands on her arms.

"No."

"If I haven't said it already, I will now. You're a lousy liar."

"It's not full-on crying. Just a tear or two." She sniffled and tried to step away.

His grip tightened and he turned her, pulling her into his arms and against his broad chest. Wrapped in his comforting embrace was probably the safest she'd ever felt in her life. How could that be when the things he made her feel were big and scary? The emotions swimming inside made her want to both run and stay.

He rubbed a hand up and down her back. "Don't cry, Maggie. Everything will be fine."

"I know. It's just—" A giant knot of emotion cut off her words.

"You're sad."

She nodded against his chest.

"You want to stay."

She nodded again.

"So don't go."

She shook her head, then permitted herself one last moment to savor the sweet, solid feel of him before stepping away. "I have to. Everything is all arranged."

"It can be unarranged. I'll call Ginger and cancel your replacement."

Brushing the moisture from her cheeks, she blew out a long breath. "Then what?"

"We go back to business as usual."

"And what happens two months from now if you change your mind? You find Ms. Right and don't need a nanny and kick me to the curb." She looked at him, the fiercely determined expression in his eyes. "What about me? That sounds incredibly selfish, but I—"

"I'll have a contract drawn up for any length of time you want. If my situation changes, I'll pay it out, no questions asked. I'll even add a rider for a bonus, proportional to time employed versus the amount of time left on the contract."

She realized he didn't get the emotional toll this was taking on her. "You think money can solve any problem?"

Without hesitation he said, "Yes."

"You're wrong, Jason. Money isn't the solution to everything."

"It doesn't necessarily buy happiness, but it can buy a way out of problems. And that may be as close to happy as a person can get."

"Money doesn't keep your heart from breaking," she protested.

"Do you love Brady?" He nudged her chin up with his knuckle, forcing her gaze to his. "Don't lie to me, Maggie. I'll know if you do. You're exceptionally bad at it."

"I guess I missed Deception 101 when I was in the convent."

"You're stalling. Do you love my son?"

Judging by the way her heart was breaking, the answer to that question was easy. "Yes."

"Then don't go. Stay and help him grow into the best person he can be."

She shook her head. "My mind is made up. There's nothing you can say to change it."

"There must be." A muscle in his jaw moved as his dark eyes turned almost black with frustration. "What if I asked you to marry me?"

She stared at him for several moments, not realizing she'd been holding her breath until she dragged air into her lungs. "That's a joke, and I'm not even going to dignify it with a response."

"Why not? I'm dead serious."

"Oh, please."

He rested his hands on lean hips, a challenging stance, as he met her gaze. There was a glitter in his eyes, as if he'd hit on the right button. "Marriage is a serious contract. It would protect your rights, something you never had in the past."

Her heart was pounding, yet it felt like all the blood had drained from her head. She couldn't think straight. He must be kidding, toying with her. And yet he looked completely determined.

"Marriage?" She held out her hands, a helpless gesture. "I don't even know how to respond to that."

"You need to come up with an answer, Maggie, because I still need one." They stared at each other and tension rolled off him in waves. "How much will it take? When you showed up, I couldn't help thinking I'd hit the jackpot. Nothing you've done has changed my opinion. I want to keep you. Name your price. How much will it take to convince you that I've never been more serious in my life? You're the answer to my prayers."

Prayer. She remembered another motherless child at Good Shepherd Home who prayed for a mother. That home was the only permanent one Maggie had ever known and it was still a haven for children. But not much longer unless Sister Margaret's prayers were getting results. She'd told Lyssa that God gives you what you need at the appropriate time.

The home needed money. A lot of it.

"Answer me, Maggie. What will it cost for you to marry me?"

She said the first thing that popped into her mind. "A million dollars."

"Done," he said without hesitation.

Chapter Five

"I don't believe you'd give me a million dollars to marry you," Maggie said.

"You don't know me very well." He stared her down. "Believe it."

When he calculated a nine-month pregnancy as opposed to raising the child for an indefinite length of time, Jason figured it was a bargain. He'd paid Catherine as much just to bring Brady into the world and she'd been giddy at the number of zeros on the bonus check simply for staying out of their lives.

Not that he wanted that greedy, grasping, self-centered woman anywhere near his son, but when he'd made the deal, he hadn't counted on the complications of caring for and bringing up a child.

Maggie's protective instincts had kicked in before she even saw Brady. She'd refused to talk until the baby was comforted and content. After Brady's first nannies, her presence these last few weeks had been like a cooling weather system from the north taking the heat off a desert summer.

Not until Maggie had walked into his life had he understood what a difference the right woman could make, in terms of child rearing. It would be stupid to let her get away, and he hadn't taken the family company to a whole new level of success by being stupid.

Maggie stared at him as if he had two heads. "I don't know whether to laugh or be afraid."

"Why?"

"*Why?*" she repeated, her voice rising. "You just offered me a large sum of money to marry you. It's like a scenario for an outrageous reality show. Or *Punk'd*." She looked up and around the room's ceiling. "Do you have cameras on me right now? Is this going on TV?"

"Don't be silly."

"Right back at you."

"On the contrary," he said, "this is the least silly idea I've ever had. It makes complete sense."

"Not to me." She folded her arms over her chest, drawing his attention there.

The only part of this idea that was silly had to do with his level of attraction. Instead of decreasing with time as he'd thought, the longer she stayed, the more appealing things he noticed about her—the subtle curves of her body that jeans only accentuated. Her high, firm breasts outlined by sweaters, blouses and T-shirts. His escalating curiosity about how her full lips would taste, how they'd feel against his own.

This was not a good time to let all that considerable appeal distract him from negotiating with her.

"Nothing about this makes sense," she said.

"Can you be more specific?"

"In this day and age men don't pay women to marry them."

"That's where you're wrong." He held up three fingers. "Three words. Anna Nicole Smith."

"Oh, please. Completely different situation. The man was ninety-something and she was after his money."

"How do you know he wasn't looking for someone to nurture his children?"

"If I remember right, his son was in his fifties or sixties. The guy could take care of himself. By any stretch of the imagination she was a gold digger."

"Maybe he was interested in companionship and was willing to pay for it. Strictly a business deal. Not unlike what I've proposed."

"How do you know I'm not a gold digger?"

The idea that she could be manipulative and calculating made him smile. "The definition of a gold digger is someone who uses her feminine wiles for gifts or monetary gain. You haven't done that. And I will have my attorney draw up a prenuptial agreement to protect me from any possible challenge to my financial assets. It would just be a precaution. Something a smart man does."

"At this particular moment, I have some serious doubts about your intelligence level. A smart man wouldn't propose this in the first place."

"He would to do right by his son. What kind of father would I be if I didn't secure the best possible future for Brady?"

"You'd sacrifice your own future for his?"

That presupposed he had a romantic future. He didn't. No woman could get close because he wouldn't let them. "I'm not sacrificing anything, Maggie."

"Because you love him."

It wasn't a question, and that pleased him. "Yes."

"A father should love his son enough to do anything for him, but that doesn't mean you *should* do anything for him."

He took a step closer, near enough to reach out and touch

her. Something he badly wanted to do again after holding her in his arms. In the mirror behind her he could see her back, the trim, ramrod straight posture. Or it could be tension. This was a big step. It should give him pause, but the more he thought about it, the more right it felt.

"Tell me something," he said. "Do you need the money? Is there something you could do with it?"

She caught the corner of her bottom lip between her teeth. "Doesn't everyone need cash?"

He looked at her and smiled. "I don't."

"Okay." She slid her fingers into the pockets of her jeans. "But the average person could use a large sum of money. If not, Las Vegas would just be a tiny town in the desert. It's built on dreams of winning big."

"And I'm offering you an opportunity to do that. It's not a dream and there's no luck involved. All you have to do is say the word. And you didn't answer my question. Is there something you could use money for?"

"Yes." She looked down and her silky hair framed her face, teased her cheeks.

His heart lurched and his hands tingled with the urge to tunnel his fingers in all that shiny hair and cup her face. "Tell me what it is."

She met his gaze. "The Good Shepherd Home is in a bad way. I told you about the building being in disrepair. Sister Margaret and Sister Mary have done everything, talked to everyone they can think of. So far the money isn't pouring in. And I don't think bake sales and car washes will make a dent in what they need."

"I've just offered you the perfect solution."

The conflict raging within her shadowed her eyes. "It's not perfect."

"Nothing ever is. But we both get what we want." He took her hands. It seemed safe enough until he felt her doubts in the trembling and the softness of her skin. But he hung on and squeezed gently, reassuringly. "You're afraid of getting emotionally attached, then losing your position as nanny. I need someone I trust with my son. If you marry me, I get what I want and you'll have a guaranteed place in my household. Another plus is the money to bail out Good Shepherd. Call it a sign-on bonus."

"If it closes, the kids will lose their home. And each other. Some of them are the only family they've got."

Like her. He'd spent a lot of years resenting the revolving door of women through his father's life and the fact that his mother walked out when he was barely old enough to remember her. But he never forgot the grief and anguish of wondering what he'd done to drive her away. Still, he'd never had to worry about a roof over his head or where he was going to live. Or who would take care of him because his father had secured the best help money could buy.

"You have the power to make a difference, Maggie. All you have to do is say yes."

Her gaze jumped to his. "Why marriage, Jason? What if I just agree to stay?"

"I want a guarantee, too. Assurance that you *will* stay. That no one will hire you away." And another thought struck him, this one more disturbing. "What if you find Mr. Right? What if some guy swoops in, sweeps you off your feet and marries you himself? I need stability for my son, and marriage does that."

Jason stared at her hands, still in his. With his thumb, he brushed her left ring finger picturing another man putting an engagement ring there, the symbol of his promise to keep her forever. The idea didn't set well.

The same instincts that made him a successful businessman should have warned him to go slowly with this proposal. Unfortunately, he didn't have that luxury. He needed to seal this deal now, while she was off balance. Before she had a chance to sleep on it and say no in the morning. If that happened, she'd walk out on her own terms. And he needed her to stay on his.

"I have to have your answer, Maggie. What's it going to be? Will you marry me?"

She pulled her hands from his and folded her arms over her chest. "Jason, I just don't—"

"As soon as you say yes, I'll write a check to Good Shepherd with a lot of zeros on it."

"You could stop payment," she pointed out.

Clearly he wasn't the only one with trust issues. "If it will make you feel better, I'll set up an account. You can have an independent attorney look over the paperwork to make sure there's nothing funny going on. I'll jump through hoops if you want, but I need an answer now. Yes or no, Maggie?"

"It does feel a lot like God putting me in the right place at the right time," she hedged.

"I'd call it a sign," he agreed. "Are you in?"

Her beautiful eyes were full of doubt but she finally said the word he wanted to hear. "Yes."

He held out his hand and hers was shaking when she settled it into his palm, signifying the agreement.

"Is everything ready to sign?" Jason looked across the desk at his attorney.

Blake Decker of Decker and Associates had handled his father's third and fourth divorces, and was currently involved in financial negotiations for dissolution of property with the most recent, soon-to-be ex-wife.

"Of course it's all ready. But a lawyer's job is also to advise. They don't call me counselor for nothing. I need to ask if you know what you're doing." The guy was in his thirties, tall, black-haired and physically fit. What women today call a hottie. And one of the city's most notoriously marriage-phobic bachelors. "What are you thinking, man?"

"I'm marrying Maggie Shepherd. What's your point?"

Blake leaned forward in his chair. "You're making a legal commitment to the nanny. It's a hell of a step to take for continuity in child care."

"Then it's a good thing you're not taking it." Jason knew exactly what he was doing. "But you're entitled to your opinion."

"My opinion is that marriage is the worst possible risk. I've never seen one work out."

"With good reason. You're a divorce attorney."

"And I'm making an unbelievable amount of money doing what I do, which goes to what I just said. Getting married is a straight shot to legal, financial and emotional complications that you don't need. Trust me. I've been through it."

"That's because you, along with most of the rest of the population, go into marriage with starry eyes and unrealistic expectations."

"And you're not?"

"Strictly business. I need someone to care for Brady. Maggie is exceptionally good at it. She's already exceeded my expectations, and your job is to safeguard the financial part. Considering the fact that you negotiate so many breakups, I figured you were the perfect guy to draft a loophole-free prenup."

"If you insist on going through with this, she won't be able to touch your assets when it blows up in your face."

"That's not going to happen. Maggie isn't like that."

"That's what all starry-eyed grooms say," Blake pointed out.

"I've never had stars in my eyes." Just the opposite. Jason figured he was born a realist and life reinforced his basic nature.

"What about emotional fallout?"

"Not a problem. We're not in love." He liked and respected Maggie. She was smart, funny and pretty in a pure, innocent way that was incredibly appealing. But love? Jason knew better than to go there. "We both have good reasons that don't include a relationship. All the cards are on the table."

"So I can't talk you out of it?"

"No."

"Don't say I didn't try." Blake shook his head and leveled a "poor bastard" look at him, then opened the file. "I have the prenuptial agreement. And the paperwork is drawn up for a million-dollar trust. I'll be the administrator for the funds that go to the Good Shepherd Home for Children."

"Good."

"Then we're ready to get all the pertinent signatures." Blake pushed the intercom button and asked the receptionist to send Maggie in.

Jason had the strangest sensation of wanting to leave before any papers were signed, but he was his father's son, a witness over the years to the worst in relationship fallout that had shaped the man he was today. No way he'd take this step without safety measures in place because marriage was like sex with a condom—sometimes it breaks. He'd seen that happen, too, and Brady was the result.

But there was something inherently sweet and unspoiled about Maggie that he didn't want tainted or shattered. Seeing the lawyer had been all about protecting his son and himself. And now he couldn't shake the feeling of wanting to protect Maggie, too, from all the sordid and sleazy aspects of why they were here.

Still, she needed money. No matter how innocent she seemed, it was always good to have safeguards in place.

Maggie and Jason sat in the back of his town car with the baby strapped in between them sound asleep. His driver was taking them to the courthouse to get married.

Married.

Margaret Mary Shepherd, abandoned baby and almost a

nun, was going to marry one of Las Vegas's wealthiest and most eligible bachelors. It was absolutely and completely surreal. Long ago she'd rigidly and deliberately put any thoughts of a wedding day out of her mind. But when rogue dreams had managed to leak through, there had always been sunshine.

Not today on her actual wedding day. It was cloudy. The forecasters were predicting rain. In the desert. It never rained in the desert. Actually, it did, but when that happened flash floods were the result.

She swallowed any misgivings and reminded herself that there was a greater good here. The home was going to get the repairs so desperately needed, and she was going to be able to stay with the baby boy she'd fallen head over heels for.

And his father?

Jason was staring out the window at the buildings going by. His profile could have been carved from any one of the rocky mountains surrounding the Vegas valley. He hadn't said anything since leaving Blake Decker's office. His lawyer was a very handsome man—in her opinion not as good-looking as Jason, but they said beauty was in the eye of the beholder. If that was true, it pointed to her having a crush on her soon-to-be husband. She supposed that was better than not being able to stand him.

As far as the pros and cons in her decision to accept his proposal, all the checkmarks stacked up on the positive side. In a town with huge hotels and resorts that were built on losses, she was getting a legal commitment that would make her a winner. She couldn't get tossed out in the cold. But that didn't mean she wasn't nervous.

"Jason?"

He turned his head, his glance dropping on the baby first. His eyes softened and a heartbreakingly tender smile lessened the craggy angles of his face. "Hmm?"

"I thought Mr. Decker was very nice." She'd felt the need

to talk, but that was a lame thing to say. There was still time for him to back out. None of that paperwork meant a thing if there were no vows.

"Blake? Nice?" He met her gaze. "I'm not sure he'd think that was a compliment."

"Why?"

"Most attorneys wouldn't consider that adjective in keeping with their job description. And Blake Decker feels that way more than most."

"But it's just a job. I'm sure he's a very nice person."

Staring at her, he shook his head slightly. "Do you really believe that?"

"Of course." She clasped her hands together. "I know lawyers are called all kinds of unflattering names. Shark. Snake. Weasel."

"You forgot barracuda."

"That, too. But it doesn't define his true nature. It's his job to know the law and advise the rest of us who don't."

A guilty look flashed into his eyes, then disappeared. Working with kids at the home she'd seen the expression a lot and was pretty good at detecting it. Although what he had to feel uncomfortable about she couldn't say.

"Here we are," he said as the car slowed to a stop. Was that relief in his voice?

Jason opened the door as she unhooked the baby's car seat. He reached back inside for the handle and lifted Brady out without waking him.

Following him up the concrete steps outside the Clark County Courthouse, her heart started to race, and it wasn't about hurrying up steps or going through the metal detectors. The official atmosphere was crystallizing. It was one thing to discuss marriage and another thing to walk into the halls of justice to speak legally binding vows.

Their footsteps echoed on the marble floor as they made

their way to the elevator that took them to the clerk's office. He'd explained this to her. In Nevada, no blood test was required, but both parties wishing to marry had to appear before the county clerk for a marriage license. After proper identification was verified, a fee of fifty-five dollars in cash was paid and a certificate allowing them to marry exchanged. Her stomach lurched, not unlike the way it reacted in the elevator.

But everything went as he'd said it would. Then she followed Jason down the hall and into a room with generic plastic chairs lined up in the middle. Jason set the still-sleeping baby down on the floor by the first row. She'd always thought that if she married, it would happen in church. She'd have been wrong. Her wedding was happening in the same building where criminals went on trial and justice was meted out. It was best not to dwell on that.

Maggie sat and looked at the other couples waiting to get married. One girl who hardly looked old enough to be here wore a strapless, long white gown. Her husband-to-be didn't look like he shaved yet. A middle-aged woman, with the portly man of her dreams, was dressed in a black-and-white suit. Maggie's beige dress with matching jacket couldn't have been more unremarkable. This wasn't an especially good time to realize she'd wanted her wedding day to *be* remarkable.

Strapless-wedding-dress girl leaned across the chair separating them and smiled. "Your baby is so precious."

Maggie started to explain that he wasn't hers, then decided not to go there. "Yes, he is. Thank you."

"I'm going to have a baby," she confided.

"Congratulations," Maggie said.

"Thanks." She looked at Jason who was speaking with the clerk. "He's pretty cute, too."

Maggie studied the dashing figure he cut in his conservative navy suit, dark hair stylishly cut and her heart pitched and rolled. "I couldn't agree more."

"You guys are an awesome family."

Did that make her "awesome" by association? Before she could answer that question, Mr. Awesome returned. "We're all set," he said, picking up the car seat.

Maggie looked around at the couples who had been there when they walked in. "All these people are ahead of us."

"Blake pulled some strings. A justice of the peace he knows pretty well managed to get us in right away."

"Don't you get thrown out of amusement parks for taking cuts in line?"

He laughed. "I told you *nice* wasn't exactly the best adjective for my attorney."

"Still, it feels wrong. Shouldn't we wait our turn?"

One dark eyebrow lifted. "Are you stalling, Maggie? Maybe you're having second thoughts?"

Second. Third. Fourth. But God had given her the means to a miracle, and now she decided it best not to think at all. "I gave my word."

He nodded. "Then let's do this."

She sighed once, then squared her shoulders and followed him through a door. The room was an office, the man before them an officer of the court.

"Fred Knox," he said, shaking hands with Jason. Then he glanced at the baby. "Nice-looking fella."

"Thanks." Jason's voice was warm with pride.

"You're here to make this family official."

Jason met her gaze. "That's the idea."

"Let's do it, then." He opened a book and settled their marriage license on it. "Do you Jason Hunter Garrett take Margaret Mary Shepherd to be your wife for richer for poorer, in sickness and in health?"

"I do."

When he repeated the words to her, Maggie said, "I do."

"Do you have rings to exchange?"

Jason reached into his jacket pocket and produced a jeweler's black-velvet box with two gold bands inside and handed them over. He'd thought of everything.

The man said, "These rings signify that love is enduring, without beginning or end."

And sometimes it's nonexistent because this marriage wasn't about love. In spite of her sound logic and self-reassurances, the thought made her sad.

Jason slipped the band on her left ring finger and it fit perfectly. His large hand dwarfed hers as she did the same, using a little effort to slide the circle of gold over his knuckle.

"With the authority vested in me by the state of Nevada, I now pronounce you husband and wife. Congratulations, Mr. and Mrs. Garrett. You may kiss your bride."

Maggie's eyes widened as her gaze shot to Jason's. She was also aware that most business deals ended with a handshake, not a kiss. Her heart was pounding, but he seemed cool and in control. His hands on her arms were strong as he drew her against him. Then he lowered his lips to hers and her eyes drifted shut. The touch of his mouth was warm and soft. His hands slid down her arms and left heat in their wake. Her heart fluttered, quick and hard. Then he pulled away and she wasn't ready for it to be over.

"That's it then," he said softly.

Was that it? She looked at him and the intensity in his eyes made her shiver with a sort of excitement that was as new and different as her marital state. Before she had a chance to guess at what he was feeling, Jason glanced at his watch.

"It's getting late. We have to go."

After congratulations and goodbyes, he took the car seat and placed his hand at the small of her back to guide her outside and to the waiting car. When they were settled inside, he gave the driver instructions to drop him at his office and take Maggie and the baby home.

"You're going to work?" she asked.

"I'm late for a meeting," he explained.

Of course he was. This was just another day at the office to him. What had she expected?

That was the thing. Until she'd taken each step and realized otherwise, she hadn't been aware of having expectations. Getting married felt like a big deal to her, but to him it was simply the first business deal of the day.

She'd never expected to be sad and disappointed on her wedding day.

Chapter Six

It was his wedding day.

"Night," Jason said to himself, something tightening inside him.

He tossed back the remainder of the Rémy Martin in his glass as he glanced around his study, noting that everything was the same. The lie echoed through him and collided with the heat that still lingered from kissing Maggie after their vows. The sensation was a lot like what happened when cold and hot air smashed together. Turbulence. Tornado.

All day he'd tried to get her off his mind. Some of it was about the bruised look in her eyes when his driver had left him at the office and Maggie realized her wedding day would be nothing out of the ordinary.

The devil of it was that there'd been nothing pressing workwise and he could have taken her someplace special for lunch. He hadn't because it was important to set a tone for the marriage. They were husband and wife in name only per their deal. What had seemed like a good idea at the time didn't look as rosy from this side of the marriage license.

Like every other night since she'd been his nanny, Maggie was bathing the baby and he was working in the study. He wanted to be with them but was keeping to his protocol of establishing a pattern. It seemed important until tension and heat ground through him.

He shot to his feet, grabbed his empty glass and went to the sideboard where he kept the cognac. After pouring another shot, he drank it down, glad for the burn in his throat and the scorching all the way to his gut. For that few seconds the scalding was all he could think about. When it subsided, there was still a vision of Maggie and the innocently seductive way she'd slid her tongue over her soft lips after he'd kissed her.

The phone rang and Jason was grateful for the distraction. "Yes?" he said into the receiver.

"Mr. Garrett, it's Peter Sexton."

The doorman. "What is it, Peter?"

"Sir, a Mr. Hunter Garrett is here to see you."

His father. "Send him up, Peter."

"Right away, sir."

The old man usually stopped by Garrett Industries corporate offices if he had something to say. This must be important. Jason had a pretty good idea what it was about.

When the bell rang, he opened the door. "Hi, Dad."

"Jason."

Hunter marched right in. "I need to talk to you."

"I figured." He shut the door. "Let's go in my study."

Jason led the way down the hall and held out a hand for his father to take one of the chairs in front of the desk. It occurred to him for the first time that the pretentious leather and gold buttons suited his father much better than his nanny. There was a resemblance between Hunter and himself, but he'd gotten his dark eyes and hair from the maternal DNA, not that he remembered much about the woman who'd birthed him. The few pictures he'd managed to find confirmed it.

The man who'd sired him was often called *distinguished* and that was fair. He was tall, and a personal trainer hammered him into fitness. Silver streaked his brown hair and his blue eyes, never brimming with warmth, were glacial at the moment.

"Would you care for a drink?" Jason asked him.

"Yes."

He poured another and set it down in front of his father before taking a chair on the other side of the desk. "How are you, Dad? How's Tracy?" Wife-to-be number five.

"Fine." The older man downed the contents of his glass, then leaned forward. "I didn't come to update you on me or my fiancée."

"Then why did you come?"

"What's going on, Jason?"

"Care to be more specific?"

"Don't be coy." For the first time Hunter's eyes were warm. Must have a lot to do with the glare. "There was a disturbing rumor on the news about the president of Garrett Industries at the Clark County Courthouse with an unidentified woman."

"I see." If his thoughts hadn't been so preoccupied with Maggie, he'd have seen this coming. Marriage licenses were public record and he didn't have an especially low profile. Someone was bound to notice. Call him perverse, but he was going to make his father work for this. He stared down the old man without saying more.

"I put in a call to Blake Decker."

"Oh?" What did that say about father-son communication that he called the attorney for information? "What did he say?"

"Nothing. He cited attorney-client privilege. That means he's your lawyer. Since when, Jason?"

"Today." Technically he'd had representation since making the call to draw up all the papers. But they'd been signed today. And he'd had his five-hundred-dollar-an-hour lecture on the potholes and pitfalls of ball-and-chain lane.

"Who's the woman?"

"Since I didn't see the news, I can't be sure who you're referring to."

Hunter's eyes narrowed. "The one at the courthouse. Who is she?"

"Her name is Margaret Mary Shepherd." Garrett, he added to himself.

"What is she to you?"

That was actually a very good question and something he'd been trying to figure out, what with the lopsided amount of time he'd been thinking about her. But he'd throw his dad a bone here. "She's Brady's nanny."

"Please don't tell me you're fooling around with the nanny."

"All right. I won't tell you."

Silver eyebrows drew together as he scowled. "Are you aware that the price of stock can rise and fall with even a hint of scandal? Hanky panky with your nanny is a very good way to get your name in the newspapers for all the wrong reasons."

His father should know. Marital escapades were his stock in trade. "Look, Dad, I'm in charge of the company now. You're chairman of the board of directors of Garrett Industries."

"I'm also your father."

"Yeah." By the tone he was assuming the old man felt the family connection gave him free rein over his life. "What's your point?"

"In this news item there was mention of a marriage license. So just why were you at the courthouse with her?"

"I married Maggie, Dad."

The old man wasn't often speechless and historically it didn't last long. "You're married? Legally?"

"Yes."

"At least you had the good sense to consult Blake."

"What? No congratulations?" Jason asked.

Without comment his father went on, "Did she sign a prenup?"

"She did." The rest of their terms were none of the old man's business.

"Good. If you made an honest woman of her there's no impropriety. No lawsuits for harassment."

"For what it's worth, the confidentiality agreement she originally signed is legally enforceable if breached. And The Nanny Network does thorough and extensive background checks on its employees."

"What is her background?"

Jason remembered Maggie's flare of temper when she assumed he was judging her for being abandoned at Good Shepherd. He decided to keep that part to himself and go with the later years. "Maggie was in the convent."

"She's a nun?" Hunter stared at him, again speechless.

"Not quite. She didn't take final vows." Jason finished the cognac in his glass.

The wheels were turning in Hunter's head and a crafty look slid into his eyes. "So she played hard to get." He nodded knowingly. "Marriage will put to rest any hint of impropriety while you fool around with her."

Anger knotted in Jason's gut. Fool around with Maggie? He wished he could say the thought never entered his mind, but since kissing her that's pretty much all he *had* thought about. And none of his thoughts were up for discussion, with his father or anyone else.

"Maggie isn't the kind of woman you fool around with, Dad."

"Maybe. But in my experience every woman has an agenda." Hunter nodded thoughtfully as he mulled that over. "Blake Decker is very good at his job, so even if she does, she can't take a chunk out of you financially in the divorce. Which is all you have to worry about." He smiled for the first time. "At least you're thinking with your head, along with other parts of your anatomy."

By association and genetics Jason felt slimy. He might think about it, but acting on impulse wasn't going to happen. He'd safeguarded his son's care and used Maggie to do it. No way would he compromise her further.

"Almost a nun." Hunter put his empty glass on the desk and stood. "I can understand the novelty. She's not your usual type."

"Yeah." And that worked both ways. He wasn't her type, either, not nearly good enough.

"Do yourself a favor, Jason." His father pointed a warning finger at him. "Don't make the mistake of falling in love."

Preaching to the choir, Jason thought. "Not a problem, Dad."

A sound in the doorway drew his attention and he saw Maggie standing there with the baby in her arms.

"You must be Maggie." Hunter studied her, then nodded his approval. "I'm Hunter Garrett."

"Jason's father." Then she looked at the baby who started to fuss. "And Brady's grandfather."

"Yes." He looked at Jason with a gleam in his eyes. "It's time for me to go. I'll leave you two alone."

He left with the same abruptness as his arrival. No congratulations or welcome to the family. No apology for dropping by on their wedding night, Jason thought darkly.

"I didn't mean to interrupt," Maggie said, staring at the closed front door. "Apparently he didn't come to see his grandson."

"That's Dad." A walking, talking cautionary role model. And his only family besides Brady.

"I brought the baby to spend time with you before he goes to bed."

"Thanks."

She settled the boy in his arms. "If he needs me, I'll be in my room."

It didn't escape his notice that she'd said if the baby needed anything. That specifically excluded Jason, which started a burning deep inside him. Why did the need for something crank up exponentially when you knew it was off-limits? He wanted her. As of this morning he had the right to have her in his bed. As his father had so indelicately put it—he could fool around with her and not worry about impropriety.

But he didn't dare touch her.

As she backed away, he noticed the same bruised look he'd seen a few minutes ago and knew she'd heard the last part of his conversation. The part where he acknowledged that he locked her into a legal relationship, confirmed that she wasn't his type and was adamant that he'd never have feelings for her. But why should it bother her? She was getting what she wanted out of the deal.

But he couldn't shake the feeling that he'd caged a butterfly. He'd never felt more like his father's son than he did now and he didn't like it one bit.

When Jason's driver dropped Maggie off in front of the home she saw Sister Margaret out front, pulling her black sweater tight against the wind. There was a truckload of— well, trucks—scattered on the property and along the street nearby. Pallets of roofing tiles and lumber waited on the cement driveway.

Maggie's footsteps crunched on the ground and the tall nun turned. Instantly a welcoming smile creased her worn face.

"Hi, Sister," she said with a wave.

"Maggie!" The nun opened her arms and gave her a big hug. "How are you?"

"Fine."

The fib was automatic, more like being economical with the truth. Mostly she was fine. Her body was functioning well, maybe a bit too well, especially when thoughts of Jason Garrett crept in and made her skin flush and her heart race. It had been more than a week since he'd kissed her at their wedding and the memory of his mouth on hers made her want more of the same. The feel of his chest pressed against her breasts made her hot and tingly all over, so her body was firing on all cylinders.

But her spirit? Not so fine. After hearing Jason tell his father that loving her was not part of his plan, her spirit had pretty much imploded. Although that information was not something she'd burden Sister Margaret with.

"How are you, Sister?"

"Excellent." She turned back to watch the workmen tearing off the rundown roof. "We're getting this old building in shape and the state granted us an extension for the work. The children have a home and all's right with the world."

"I'm glad."

Sister looked down at her. "Without the generous donation from your Mr. Garrett none of this would be possible."

Maggie opened her mouth to say he wasn't hers, but decided more truthful economy was indicated. As far as the state of Nevada was concerned, he *was* hers. Legally her husband. At his luxurious penthouse, she would never be his wife, only the nanny. As guilty as it made her feel to withhold facts, Sister Margaret did not need to know she'd married Jason for his donation. And he'd married her to ensure her loyalty to his child.

She didn't want to see the disappointment in Sister's eyes when she confessed to marrying the man for his money, no matter how well intentioned she'd been.

"And there's more," Sister continued.

Maggie wasn't sure her guilty conscience could handle more. She pulled her Windbreaker around her as a gust of cold blasted her. With clouds covering the sun, it was very chilly. Or maybe that was just the freeze in her heart.

"What else did Jason do?" she asked.

"He took care of getting bids on the renovations. I spoke with him myself and—"

"You talked to Jason?" *Oh, good Lord.* Did he say anything about their arrangement?

Sister nodded. "He's quite a charming man. Very nice phone voice."

He was even nicer to look at, Maggie thought, but kept the information to herself. And she knew all about that whiskey-and-chocolate voice. Somehow he'd used it to talk her into this arrangement. But if she was being honest, it had taken precious little effort on his part to convince her this arrangement would work.

"Jason is many things positive," she agreed.

"After helping us out with the donation I didn't want to take up his time with those details, but he insisted. He assured me that in his business dealings through Garrett Industries he has many contacts and finding the right company to do the work for us would be easier for him."

"He's built some pretty spectacular resorts here in Las Vegas."

"Does he talk about that?"

"We mostly talk about the baby." *His* baby, Maggie silently added. But every day Brady felt more like hers and she let herself go there. Because of the marriage, she wasn't going to lose him. "I've read about his work in the *Review Journal*. I read aloud to the baby." She shrugged. "It's never too early to start reading to a child."

"I can't argue with that. And speaking of arguing, when I tried to do that with Mr. Garrett, he asked whether or not I wanted to get the best quality construction for a rock-bottom price." Sister laughed. "Only an idiot would have said no to that."

"And you're one smart cookie, Sister," Maggie said.

"Before I knew it, the roofing company called and scheduled the job, and here they are. Next up are renovations to the plumbing. Also thanks to your Mr. Garrett. A crew will be available when this part of the project is complete. Which shouldn't be more than a week." She looked up at the threatening sky. "And with help from the good Lord, we will not get rain until after our brand-new roof is in place. Gus said that—"

"Gus?"

"The man in charge," Sister explained. "He said the job will take several days. Demolition—that's taking off the old roof—will be the most time-consuming part. Because of the weather they'll put plastic over it. But I'm thinking we might want to move the children in those upstairs rooms just to be safe."

"Okay. I'm here to help however you need me," Maggie assured her.

Sister draped an arm around her shoulders. "You're a blessing from God."

That was something Sister had said as far back as Maggie could remember, but now it felt different. She was glad that she'd been in the right place at the right time to make God's plan happen for this very special home. But she knew, as surely as she knew the thermometer would hit triple digits in July, that if Sister was aware of the facts behind this donation, she would not consider it a blessing. And that's why she could never find out.

Maggie would do anything to keep the smile on this woman's face. Including a lie of omission.

"We also have to keep the children inside and away from the workmen for their own safety."

"I understand."

"Sister Mary and another volunteer took a group of older kids to the movies. We received some free passes and the timing couldn't have been better. The little ones will be easier to look after inside."

"Okay." Maggie linked her arm through Sister's as they walked toward the house. "We'll keep them busy."

"You can read aloud from the newspaper," Sister teased.

"I promise you they'll love it," Maggie said.

"I'm sure they will. Sweetie, you could read the phone book and have them eating out of your hand. You've always had a way with the little ones." On the covered porch Sister Margaret stopped and took in the sight of the workmen. "It's so important to give them a positive start in life."

"I absolutely agree." Wasn't she doing that with Brady? She was grateful for the chance to give him all the tender, loving care he needed for a positive start in his little life.

"I want to do more, Maggie." Sister looked down at her. "This donation is so extraordinarily generous. With Mr. Garrett's help it will go further than just the repairs. There will be money left over for unexpected expenses. Or maybe a scholarship for someone who might not otherwise be able to go to college."

"That's wonderful, Sister." She'd struggled with money while getting her education. It would be fantastic to ease the way for an exceptional student with limited resources.

"It's a gift that will keep on giving."

Maggie looked at the woman beside her, the genuine happiness she felt at being given the means to smooth the way for others. Maybe even more good would come out of the deal she'd made. She'd always felt that she got a miracle the night the sisters found her on this very porch and took her in. Through The Nanny Network, God had put her in the right place, in Jason Garrett's path, so that she could pay her miracle forward.

She hoped so because personally this deal had landed her right in purgatory. It was a state of temporary misery where a soul could make up for past sins and earn a pass to heaven. She'd been taught that it was a condition where one could see what they were missing out on but not participate.

By that definition, she was definitely in purgatory. She had a front-row seat of what a family of her own could look like, a clear view of what she'd always wanted. But it wasn't actually hers.

She'd had a wedding, but no wedding night. And the more time she spent with Jason, the more her body felt the emptiness, the more she yearned to be his wife in every sense of the word.

He was a good man, a man she respected more every day. For the sake of the child he loved more than anything, he'd married a woman he could never love. Somehow she'd have to make peace with what she'd done.

She'd have to find a way to live with seeing what she wanted every single day, all the while knowing she couldn't ever really have it.

Chapter Seven

Practically from the first moment Maggie had walked into his life Jason was aware of her in all the wrong ways. Tonight was no exception, unless you counted him wanting her more. That probably had something to do with feeling her absence. Not because flying solo with his son was an inconvenience. Just the opposite. He cleared his schedule without hesitation to make time for Brady. The more time he spent with him, the more confident he felt. But the penthouse had seemed so empty while she'd been gone doing her duty at the home.

That's the thing. He couldn't find a shred of a clue that she considered what she did a duty. Instead she only talked about what she got out of helping and felt selfish for getting anything at all. That purity of spirit was a big part of why he couldn't get her off his mind. He'd never known a woman like her.

With an almost soundly sleeping Brady pressed to his chest, Jason walked the floor in the living room as he looked at the bright lights of Las Vegas below him. Maggie had returned this afternoon. Normally she was perky and chatty and full of stories about the children and activities at Good Shepherd. Today she seemed troubled.

And how long had it been since he'd actually been aware of a woman's mood?

"Never." When Brady squirmed in his arms, Jason gently patted his back and made the shushing noise Maggie had taught him. "Sorry, pal," he said softly.

He continued to move until the baby completely relaxed, a sign that he was sound asleep. After walking down the hall into the nursery, he settled Brady on his back and gently brushed the dark hair from his forehead as tiny lips pursed and sucked in sleep.

A tenderness unlike any emotion he'd ever known welled up inside Jason as he pulled the blanket up to his child's waist. He wouldn't stay covered long because he was really moving around a lot, getting bigger every day. Maggie had informed him that soon Brady would be rolling from his back to his stomach. Amazing how much had changed since Maggie had come into their lives.

Including the fact that she was his wife, Jason thought.

His body went tight with need. Wasn't life ironic? He'd never been without a woman when he was a single man. Now that he had a baby and a wife, regular sex was a distant memory.

After sliding the baby monitor in the back pocket of his jeans, he walked out of the nursery. In the hallway, he heard sounds of the treadmill coming from his home gym. He'd bought an elliptical trainer, free weights and treadmill for the convenience of a home workout and not taking time away from his son. In the evening, while he and Brady hung out, it had become her habit to use the equipment.

Work waited in his study but he was too restless and distracted for spreadsheets and reports. Knowing it was probably a stupid move, he headed in the other direction.

The door was open and Maggie was walking briskly on the treadmill, her back to him. She was wearing a tank top and knit pants, both of which clung to the curves he'd been dreaming about, shifting his body into high gear. Instantly he had a mental picture of those shapely legs wrapped around his waist while he was buried deep inside her.

She was the one exerting herself, but sweat popped out on his forehead. He'd swear he hadn't made a sound, but only moments after he'd stopped in the doorway she looked over her shoulder and surprise registered in her expression.

"Jason?" She placed her feet on either side of the moving tread, then slid the speed lever to off so the machine slowed and finally stopped. "Is Brady all right?"

"Fine. He's asleep."

She grabbed the small towel draped over the handrail and wiped the moisture from her face.

The view from the front was just as good as the back, maybe better. The brief tank was moist and clung to her small, firm breasts. His skin felt too tight and his nerve endings were tingling. He was probably giving off some kind of electrical humming sound, which could explain how she'd known he was there. Or it could have been a moan, something he wouldn't have heard because of the blood rushing from his head to points south.

She blew out a breath and brushed the dark hair off her forehead. "This is early for him to go down. Maybe I better check to see if he's really settled."

"Take five. I've got the baby monitor. We'll know if sleep is a false alarm. My son isn't shy about letting his needs be known."

"I've noticed." The words were light and teasing, but her normal smile was missing in action.

"Is something wrong, Maggie?"

"No." Her gaze jumped to his. "Why?"

"You've been uncharacteristically quiet since you got back from Good Shepherd today. Did something happen?"

Turning away, she walked over to the elliptical machine and grabbed the sweatshirt hanging there. After pulling it over her head, she slid her arms in and pulled it down. The bulky garment hid even more of her skin and the curves that made his body tighten with need and ache to touch her. He very nearly reached out to tug the damn thing off, but resisted the urge, just barely, by sliding his fingers into the pockets of his jeans.

Maggie met his gaze. "There are lots of things happening at the home."

That didn't answer his question. "Define lots of things."

"Workmen were there ripping off the roof. Out with the old, in with the new."

"Good."

"Sister Margaret tells me when that job is finished, there's a plumbing crew waiting to make the necessary repairs and upgrades."

"Excellent."

"Yes, it is." She draped the towel around her neck.

"And yet you look as if there's something not right."

"Do I? Everything feels fine."

Not in his skin. But he wasn't about to share that. His household was in place and rocking the boat would be an incredibly dumb thing to do.

He reached out and brushed a dark strand of hair from her forehead, much as he'd done with Brady just a few minutes ago. "Really?"

She nodded, then swallowed hard. "It was very nice of you to get bids and line up building contractors for Sister Margaret."

Very nice. She thought his lawyer was nice. It wouldn't surprise him if she could find redeeming qualities in Attila the Hun. As far as adjectives, he'd have much preferred studly.

Athletic. Long lasting. And just like that his mind was right back in the sack.

He swallowed the need as best he could. "I know people. It wasn't a problem."

"Still, you're a busy man. Taking the time to help was very gracious of you."

Very gracious? More bland adjectives that made him feel sexless.

"The very least I could do to make sure no one took advantage."

"Sister Margaret wanted me to be sure and thank you. It's much appreciated. The kids and the nuns are incredibly grateful."

"What about you, Maggie?"

"Me?" She looked surprised, confused, doubtful. And incredibly beautiful. The pulse at the base of her throat fluttered wildly.

"Yes, you. Do the renovations meet with your approval?"

"If it means that the home will stay open, I absolutely approve of everything." Her chin lifted a notch as she met his gaze.

"I'm glad. Because truthfully, I've never met anyone at the home. When I made those phone calls to line up contractors, it was all about you."

"Me?"

"It's my way of thanking you for everything you've done."

"You put a million dollars in trust for something I care deeply about. We both got what we wanted. I don't understand why you went above and beyond to help."

That made two of them. He wasn't the only selfish bastard in the world, but definitely somewhere near the top. Having a child had shown him, for the first time in his life, what it was like to care about someone other than himself. And Maggie was important to his son. That's all it was about. That's all he'd let it be about. This was not a good time to have doubts about their business arrangement.

"Call it a bonus," he said. "To put the smile back on your face."

The corners of her mouth curved up and suddenly all the effort was worth it. "That wasn't necessary. But thank you."

"You're welcome."

She stared up at him, then blinked and moved toward the door. "I—I better go check on Brady. See if he needs me."

Jason needed her. Just to talk. To laugh. To fill up the emptiness inside him. Just a little longer.

He curved his fingers around her arm to stop her. "Wait, Maggie—"

She looked up at him, her eyes wide pools of innocence that drowned his willpower. He drew her against him, cupping her cheek in his hand.

"Maggie," he whispered again.

She opened her mouth to say something, but before she could he touched his mouth to hers. The soft sweetness of her lips was more intoxicating than the pricey liquor he kept in his office down the hall. Desire ground through him and knotted in his gut. He slid his hand beneath the bulky sweatshirt and settled it on her lower back, just above the curve of her butt, and pressed her more firmly against him.

Some vague instinct warned him to go slow and he fought the need to kiss her hard and possessively. He nibbled the corners of her mouth and felt her heart pounding against his own. Dropping small kisses on her cheek, then her chin and finally her neck, made her shiver and moan. When he stopped at a sensitive place just beneath her ear, she shuddered. Then he licked the responsive spot and blew softly until her groan echoed inside him. The sound sent arrows of need through him and his body tightened in response. Blood pounded in his veins and his chest felt like it would explode. The sound of Maggie's ragged breathing turned him on like he'd never been turned on before. She wanted him as much as he wanted her. For God's sake, she was his wife.

"I need you, Maggie," he whispered, his breath stirring her hair. His voice was ragged with desire.

He was about to scoop her into his arms when she pulled her mouth from his and stared at him, breathing hard. Something dark pushed the innocence from her eyes.

"What's wrong?" he asked.

"I don't want to be a novelty."

"Excuse me?" He was struggling to draw air into his lungs and that kiss blew his mind. There wasn't much left to take in and decipher a remark from out of left field.

"Your father said I was a novelty. 'Almost a nun' was different for you."

"Don't pay any attention to my father—"

"You mean the part where he was proud of you for protecting yourself financially? The part where he was pleased that you were thinking with your head as well as—other parts of your body? You planned ahead for a plaything. Offered marriage so stock prices wouldn't go down because of a scandal with the nanny."

"You know that's not how it was," he said, anger burning as hot as desire had only moments before.

"It's all about Brady, I know. But he's asleep now. Technically I'm off duty, or at least on a break. But you just kissed me."

"That's not breaking news." He couldn't deny it. Her lips were still moist from the touch of his own. But when a Garrett was backed into a corner he came out fighting. "I started it. And you kissed me back."

"It was a knee-jerk reaction." She stared at him for several moments, still breathing hard. "I'm not asking for love."

"You heard that, too?"

"Oh, yeah." Her frown pushed out any hint of sunshine, and it was his fault. "Just so we're clear, that's the last thing I'm looking for. But I will not be disrespected."

"That was never my intention," he assured her.

When he'd kissed her, he'd been thinking with his hormones, which were in perfect working order. Before she could argue that point, a sound came from his back pocket where he'd put the monitor.

"It's Brady. Break's over," she said. "I have to go to him."

"Right."

She hurried out of the room, and when she was gone, Jason felt her absence again. But this time it was all about the ache shooting through him.

He knew when it subsided he would be relieved that he hadn't taken Maggie to his bed. But right now he couldn't feel the blessing and struggled for logic.

Sleeping with her would have been a huge mistake. Sex was a complication that would destroy everything he'd so carefully put in place.

But he had to wonder what sin he'd committed. What transgression was so wicked that he was being punished by this gut-twisting desire for the one woman he didn't dare touch?

Masculine and sexy sat on Jason Garrett like a cloak and crown. Maggie had been enveloped in it last night and wanted more. She'd barely managed to break away before willingly becoming another one of his playthings. It made her wonder again about Brady's mother, but no matter how Jason had treated her, there was no way to reconcile abandoning her baby. If Brady was hers, Maggie knew there would be no walking away. He wasn't her biological child and she couldn't walk away. But there was also the small matter of the marriage to his father.

Although being driven around was a darn nice perk of the marriage, she thought, watching palm trees and buildings go by. Jason's driver had picked Maggie and Brady up from the penthouse. She sat in the back with the baby in his car seat, sound asleep beside her. The movement always did that to him. Jason had forgotten his briefcase and she'd needed the car for errands. She'd told his secretary she would swing by the office and drop it off while they were out. And, of course, the woman had said she was dying to see the baby.

Her heart seemed to expand in her chest when she smiled at the infant, probably the only person on the planet who could make her smile this morning. After what happened the night before, specifically THE KISS—all capital letters.

She wasn't so innocent that she didn't know he'd wanted her. If only the feeling wasn't mutual, but she'd be lying if she said that. Sleeping with Jason would complicate her already complicated life, but every part of her had tingled and begged to finally know what it felt like to be with a man. And not just any man.

Jason Garrett was the man she wanted. It couldn't be explained away by the fact that she hadn't been kissed in a very long time—before she'd entered the convent—by her disastrous first love. She hadn't slept with him and there'd been no one since. Technically that meant she'd saved herself for the man she married.

Silly her. When he'd dangled a million dollars in front of her, she hadn't inquired what he expected of her as his wife. Jason had been gone when she got up with Brady this morning. Now she had to face him for the first time after that kiss. In front of other people. Just goes to show that God had a sense of humor.

After exiting the 215 Beltway onto Green Valley Parkway, the car pulled into a business complex, then stopped in front of a multistoried building. As soon as the movement ceased, Brady's eyes popped open.

"This is it, Mrs. Garrett."

For a nanosecond, she thought the driver was talking to someone else. "Thanks, Martin. I'll only be a few minutes."

"Want to leave the little guy with me while you run the briefcase up to Mr. G?"

"I appreciate that, but his father wants to show him off."

Maggie had the baby in one hand and the briefcase in the other when she walked into the Garrett Industries building. Her sneakers squeaked on the lobby's marble floor as she headed for the elevator. After entering, she set both her burdens down and pushed the button for the eighth floor where Jason's office was located.

The elevator opened right into the reception area and a half-circle cherrywood desk that sat in the center of the room. Behind it was a redhead in her twenties wearing a headset for answering the phone.

When a muted ring sounded, she pushed a button and said, "Garrett Industries, Mr. Garrett's office. This is Chloe. How can I help you?" She listened for a moment and said, "Let me transfer you to customer service. Hold on, please."

Chloe De Witt. Jason's secretary. They'd talked just a little while ago.

Maggie stopped in front of the desk. "Hi. I'm—" She was going to say Margaret Mary Shepherd. But she wasn't anymore. She was Maggie Garrett, although she had no idea who Maggie Garrett was. With the very efficient secretary staring at her this was no time for an identity crisis. "I'm Maggie."

"Hi." Chloe flashed a professional smile, then disconnected her headset from the phone and came around the desk. She was wearing a snug gray pinstriped skirt and long-sleeved white blouse tucked into the waistband. The four-inch black spiked heels made her slender legs look a mile long. Her thick auburn hair was stylishly cut and brushed her silky collar. She was pretty enough to be a model. Or a show girl. Either or both of which were probably Jason's type.

After a quick glance at her own dark denim pants and red pullover sweater, Maggie felt like the peasant from Plainville, a drab and uninteresting dweeb.

Chloe saw the briefcase on the floor beside Brady's car seat. "You brought it. And this must be Jason's little guy."

"Brady."

When he heard his name, he flashed a wide smile and Chloe did a big "aww." "He is absolutely adorable."

"Yes, he is," Maggie agreed, smiling down at the incredibly cute little guy.

Could she be any more proud if he'd been her biological child? she wondered. That didn't seem possible. She was married to his father, but didn't have the right to claim him as her son. She was just the nanny.

Male voices drifted to them from down the hall. Before she saw him, Maggie heard Jason's voice.

"Chloe, do you have that paperwork yet?" The man who belonged to that familiar voice strode into the reception area with another man and spotted her. "That would be a yes. Hi, Maggie."

"Hi. I had some errands in The District, so I offered to drop off your briefcase." His cool, confident expression gave no clue how he felt about seeing her there.

"You met my secretary," he said, glancing between the two of them.

Chloe looked at him and it was clear from the adoring expression on her face that she had a serious crush on her boss. Maggie felt a tug of something unpleasant right in her midsection.

"Your son is just about the cutest thing I've ever seen," Chloe said.

Jason smiled down at the baby. "You'll get no argument from me."

"That's a first." It was the man with Jason. He was tall, about the same height, with dark hair and incredibly blue eyes. In a dark charcoal-gray suit, black shirt and geometric tie in shades of silver, he looked like a pirate, a modern-day corporate one—handsome and dashing, a scoundrel and a rogue. "But I haven't met the lady."

"Imagine that." Jason's words were laced with sarcasm and the tone squeezed out any hint of friendly banter. His eyes darkened to almost black as he frowned. "A woman in Las Vegas that you haven't met."

"What can I say?" The man's grin was unapologetic. "I'm a people person."

"Is that what you call it?" This semi-hostile Jason was a side he'd kept hidden.

"Women are people, too." He glanced at her. "Aren't you going to introduce me?"

"This is Maggie," Jason said grudgingly.

The stranger held out his hand. "I'm Nathaniel Gordon. Jason and I are working on a business deal together."

Maggie would bet Jason wasn't offering him a large sum of money to take care of his child. That was the only business deal she knew anything about. Of the four of them, five if you included Brady, she was the only one clueless about the business world. Taking that even further, she didn't have a whole lot of world experience in general. But one could never go wrong being polite.

"Nice to meet you," she said, putting her fingers in his. Brushing a strand of hair off her face, she saw that his gaze zeroed in on the plain gold band on her left ring finger. Jason noticed, too, if the muscle jerking in his taut jaw was anything to go by.

"The papers I needed are in here." He picked up the brief-case. "Let's go back to my office, Nate. I'm not finished getting the best of you yet."

"In your dreams, pal." He leveled an appreciative gaze in Maggie's direction. "It was a pleasure, Maggie."

Jason turned away. "Chloe, hold my calls for the next hour."

"An hour?" Nate followed him. "It won't take that long for me to get the upper hand in this negotiation."

Then the phone rang, and Chloe rounded the desk to plug herself back in. "Thanks for bringing the papers, Maggie. And the baby." She answered the call and waggled her fingers in a goodbye gesture.

Maggie stood by herself. This office and the professional atmosphere with its high-powered and attractive business players made her feel like she'd stepped into an alternate universe. This Jason was a man she'd seen before, driven and focused. He'd tried to be that way the first time they met, but concern for his infant son had stripped away the edges.

Here the edges were even sharper. He was cool, calm, in control. The boss. Last night, for the heart-stopping moments when his mouth had greedily taken hers, he'd been her husband.

Maggie took the elevator down, then walked to the car where Martin opened the door. She strapped the baby's car seat in and slid in beside him.

In the two months she'd known him, Jason had never forgotten the work he'd invariably brought home with him. Not ever. She wanted to believe today's anomaly happened because he'd been as bewildered by that kiss as she was. And although she desperately wanted to believe in miracles, she couldn't quite get herself to buy that one. It was easier to believe that his father was right and she was a novelty, a plaything.

The whole time she'd been in his office he'd only introduced her as Maggie and left out what she was to him. He'd never once called her his wife. She'd saved herself for the man she married, but up until that kiss she'd figured the man she married didn't want her as anything but the nanny.

Seeing him in his world, it was clear that she wouldn't fit in as anything *but* the nanny. He'd said part of the reason he insisted on marriage was to prevent another man from swooping in and marrying her.

She hadn't really bought into that, but he wasn't joking.

He didn't want her, but he didn't want anyone else to have her, either. This wasn't purgatory.

It was a deal with the devil.

Chapter Eight

Jason loved this cabin in Lake Tahoe.

When he was about eight his father had bought the place with views of the water. Every year they came here during ski season and hung out—just the two of them. Because of the parade of women through Hunter's life, the Garretts didn't have many traditions. But this was one he wanted for himself and Brady.

And Maggie.

Out of nowhere that thought popped into his mind as he watched her play with the baby. The two of them were on the thick beige carpet in front of the fire in the big stone fireplace. Sitting on the overstuffed leather corner group, Jason smiled when she kissed the baby's belly and made him laugh. It was so incredibly normal, so amazingly down-to-earth. An unfamiliar and unexpected sensation of contentment swept over him, a warm feeling that expanded and chased out the emptiness. Loneliness was another name for it, but he never felt that way when he was with Maggie.

They'd slipped back into a relaxed give-and-take, for which he was grateful. That meant he hadn't screwed things up by kissing her. Clearly she hadn't held it against him. He wished he could keep from holding it against *her,* more important, forget about it. And he'd thought a change of scene might help. So far he'd been wrong about that, but they'd only arrived a couple hours ago. She hadn't said much.

"So what do you think?"

"About?"

"This change in scenery." His gaze settled on her mouth and he knew there'd been no progress in the ongoing battle to take his mind off kissing her.

"If you're asking about the ride in your Gulfstream, I think it was—" She hesitated, obviously struggling for an appropriate adjective. "It was pretty awesome."

"Yeah. It's good being me." He laughed when she made a face at him. "But that's not what I meant. How do you like the cabin?"

She met his gaze, then looked around. "Calling it a cabin is like saying that jet is an airplane. McMansion is more to the point."

"You think?" he asked, studying the log walls and high-beam ceiling. "It's only six thousand square feet."

"That much? Feels smaller," she murmured, then handed the baby a stuffed toy that went straight into his mouth.

"You don't like it?"

Her expression was wry. "It's fantastic, and I think you're just fishing for compliments."

"I didn't realize you knew me that well," he teased.

"This is a wonderful spot," she said, not commenting on understanding him. "It's too bad this trip is just a few days. Leaving will be hard." She crossed her legs Indian style and looked at him. "Speaking of this long weekend, I'm surprised you could get away from the office with a big business deal pending."

"Deal?" He was only half-listening, enjoying the sight of her with his son. It was almost bedtime and the little guy was bathed, in pajamas and ready for the sack. The idea of being just with Maggie sent anticipation buzzing through him.

"Aren't you the relaxed one?" she commented.

"Hmm?"

"You're not listening. Either your ears don't work in higher altitudes, or when you're this far from the office you go on autopilot." She tilted her head to the side and studied him. "Or both."

"Guilty. On both counts. This place seems to give me back my serenity." And then some. She looked extraordinarily beautiful with the glow of the fire behind her and his child at her knee. He slid his hands into the pockets of his jeans and stretched his long legs out in front of him. Trying to relax, though suddenly his whole body was tight and tense. Desire throbbed through him and the vibrations were like an electromagnetic pulse that short-circuited brain function. "I'm sorry. What were you saying?"

"That I was surprised you could get out of town with a deal in the works. The one you were involved in when I was there the other day to drop off your briefcase."

"Nate Gordon."

"Yes." She glanced at him, absently holding Brady's foot and rubbing her thumb across the bottom. "How's that going?"

Of all the people he did business with, why did she have to meet Nathaniel Gordon, entrepreneur and playboy? The guy discarded women like tissues. He'd asked a lot of questions about Maggie, and Jason hadn't been prepared for it. Every answer he gave just made Nate more curious about their connection. Finally, the remark about getting Maggie's phone number because she was a babe really got Jason steamed.

He'd blurted out that she was his wife, which led to more

interrogation. Like why he was keeping her under wraps. Why hadn't he received an invitation to the biggest society wedding of the year? He'd thought they were friends, etc.

Finally Jason put a lid on the whole thing with a question of his own. Did he want to do business or start a new career as a tabloid journalist?

"Jason?"

He looked at her. "Sorry. Altitude auditory malfunction again."

"Very funny." She smiled as he'd hoped. "How's that deal working for you?"

"It looks like we'll be merging into the largest development company in Las Vegas."

"Congratulations. That sounds pretty impressive."

"It's okay."

She tilted her head and studied him. "Not impressive?"

It might have been. Probably still was. But Jason's opinion of Nathaniel Gordon did a 180 when he showed an interest in Maggie. He didn't like the way Nate had looked at her. Like she was a ripe strawberry ready for picking.

"From a business perspective it will benefit both our companies."

When Brady started making unhappy noises because he'd dropped the stuffed toy, she handed him a brightly colored set of plastic keys, which he managed to grab and shove in his mouth.

"Really?"

"Stock prices will soar. It's a smart business deal."

"Then why do you look like someone stole your Black-Berry?"

He stared at her for a moment. Was she a mind reader? Strawberry? BlackBerry? He didn't like the idea of Nate poaching anything of his. He wondered if "almost a nun" meant that Maggie had a direct line to God. If so, he'd have to be careful because what he'd been thinking wasn't up for discussion with her.

But maybe this was an opportunity. "As far as business, there's no one sharper or more successful than Nate Gordon."

"Including you?"

"Except for me." He grinned and she returned it. "We met in college and hit it off. Our strengths and weaknesses complement each other and we'd make a formidable team in developing new projects."

"Then I'm not sure I understand the problem."

"It's personal." He folded his arms over his chest. "He's not the kind of guy who puts down roots."

"Is that a delicate way of saying he has commitment issues?"

"I wouldn't know about that. All I can tell you is that if you follow the trail of Las Vegas broken hearts it will lead straight to his door."

"So he's never been married?"

"Absolutely not."

"No children?"

"Not that I'm aware of," he said.

She put her hand on the baby's belly. "Until Brady, you just described yourself."

"That was a low blow," he said, indignant.

The little guy started to fuss. Instantly she picked him up and settled him to her shoulder, patting his back. "I'm just stating facts. Now you have a son, which forces you to plan ahead for your fun and maybe you're the tiniest bit jealous of Nate."

"You couldn't be more wrong." Anger curled through him. He might be jealous but it had nothing to do with his son.

"Then why did you marry me, Jason?" She held up a hand when he started to answer. "I know how the spin goes. It's for Brady. I was there, remember? I was also there for the father-son chat about appearances. Any hint of hanky panky and stock prices take a nose dive."

"What's your point?"

"How can business be affected by what you do when no one besides your father knows we're married?"

"Nate knows," he said, but didn't volunteer the circumstances of the interrogation that had dragged out the information.

"Does Chloe?" she challenged. When he didn't answer, she nodded. "I thought so. You told Nate because it was a territorial thing. Sort of a primal, Neanderthal, don't-take-what's-mine, pounding your chest kind of posturing."

"You're calling me a caveman?"

"So not the point," she said with a sigh. "We're married."

"I was there, remember?" He winced at how childish it was to throw her own words back at her.

"We have a legal commitment. But I'm trying to figure out what that means. All I am is Maggie. When I met your secretary, there was no qualification of what I am to you. I'm not sure what my life is anymore."

"Do you want out of the agreement?"

She stood with the baby in her arms and the fire's glow backlit her slender shape and womanly curves. It was a sight that knotted his gut and practically made him salivate. If he really was a Neanderthal, he'd carry her upstairs and have his way with her. His willpower was shaky, but he was trying to be noble here. She wasn't making it easy.

"What does that mean?"

"An annulment." Since there'd never been anything physical between them.

"The money you put in trust is already being spent. You know I can't afford to pay you back."

He wouldn't make her do that. To him it was chump change. A tax write-off. "Then what do you want?"

"I don't know." The baby started to cry in earnest and she pressed him closer to her, rubbing his back and brushing her palm over his head. "I want to go home."

Just a little while ago she'd thought this trip was too short and wanted to stay longer. He'd spoiled the mood, which made him feel like the caveman she'd accused him of being.

"We'll go back in the morning."

"Okay." Her tone said it couldn't be too soon for her and so did the troubled expression in her eyes when she met his gaze. A moment later she hurried past him and upstairs with the unhappy baby.

Jason brooded as he stared at the fire. This was a hell of a mess he'd gotten himself into.

Talk about not thinking it through. He'd been so focused on closing the deal and getting her to stay, he hadn't even considered the other things that marriage meant.

Companionship.

Intimacy.

Sex.

He stood and paced in front of the fire, feeling the warmth on his skin. The heat he felt inside was all for Maggie. He wanted her.

She was his wife, for God's sake. In some odd way thoughts of sex had made him mention *annulment*. To her, that was more ammunition to prove that he'd planned ahead to play her. The truth was he hadn't planned ahead for anything. He hadn't thought about her having a life, being a wife.

But he was thinking about it now. And not with his head.

Maggie stared out the window where the swiftly falling snow covered the road and piled up outside. Ordinarily she'd have been entranced by its beauty. Snow wasn't something a resident of Las Vegas saw every day. It got cold, but not usually cold enough to snow. The sight should have been magical. But when you wanted to escape back to the real world and Mother Nature decided to make the road to the airport too icy for travel, it felt like a cosmic joke at her expense. Be careful what you wish for, because now she had to spend another night in the romantic McMansion.

"It's a blizzard," she said, stating the obvious.

"I know." Jason's tone was grim.

Wasn't it amazing how much tension six thousand square feet could contain? After their angry words last night, the strain had been palpable all day as they went out of their way to avoid each other, all the while watching the snow falling faster, burying any hope of traveling home by tonight.

Fortunately baby Brady was blissfully unaware of the edginess in the adults around him. His routine of eating, playing, napping and now down for the night had remained unchanged, which made him the only happy camper in the cabin.

She glanced over her shoulder at Jason. "This is the beginning of April, for goodness' sake. How can there be weather-related travel delays in the beginning of April?"

He folded his arms over his chest. "Did you ever hear of the Donner Party?"

Eyes wide, she turned to face him full on. "There's no food here? Brady needs formula. And—"

"Don't panic." He held up his hands. "We have rations. I just meant that freak snowstorms happen in the mountains. If I'm not mistaken, the Donner Party got caught in October, which was early for winter. We're looking at spring and it's late in the season, but snow happens."

She cocked her thumb over her shoulder toward the window and visual proof. "I noticed."

"Obviously we're not going anywhere tonight. Might as well make the best of it. I think I'll open a bottle of wine." Without waiting for a comment, he walked away.

Maggie heard noise in the kitchen, the amazing kitchen with an oblong island big enough to land his Gulfstream. The sound of drawers and cupboards opening and closing drifted to her.

She didn't know what to do with herself. Wouldn't you

think a place this size would be big enough to lose yourself in? Growing up she'd always had to share a room with one or more girls. Then she did live-in child care and a room of her own came with the territory. Along with a broken heart. She'd never existed anywhere as spacious as Jason's penthouse and this beautiful, homey, woodsy cabin. Yet with him in it, she'd never experienced an area with less breathing room. Suddenly the walls seemed to close in on her and she opened the front door and stepped into the cold on the porch.

She moved to the edge, where she knew four steps descended to the yard and the lake that was normally visible through the trees. Now, the big, wet, white flakes hid everything, including the steps. The wind blew toward her and with it the snow, stinging her cheeks. She crossed her arms over her chest against the bitter cold and started to shiver. If she could stand it out here long enough, maybe Jason would be upstairs in the fabulous master bedroom and out of sight when she was forced to go in.

The front door creaked open behind her. "Maggie?"

"Nice out here," she murmured.

"It's a blizzard," he said, echoing her words.

"I've never seen a blizzard before."

"Watching it inside would be warmer and a much better environment from which to enjoy the view."

With him around there was no such thing as a bad view. And that was why she wanted to leave. This wasn't normal. Normal consisted of him going to work. Spending hours at the office, before coming home late and giving Brady his undivided attention until the baby went to bed and she could hide in her room. It was snatches of moments with him. Not this concentration of time where she was exposed to his powerful brand of magnetism. She'd made it clear to him that respect was important to her, but how could she respect herself when she'd chewed him out for kissing her at the same time she yearned for him to kiss her again?

"I'm fine," she lied. "Who knows when I'll get another chance to experience snow up close and personal?"

He moved right behind her, close enough for her to feel the heat of his body. With every fiber of her being she longed to lean into his warmth and not just because she was freezing her tuchas off. If she stayed out long enough, maybe the blizzard would numb her to the effects of prolonged exposure to Jason's appeal.

He put his hands on her arms. "You're shivering."

"I'm f-fine."

"The sound of your teeth chattering will wake Brady."

"Not likely. Must be something about the air and altitude. He's slept better up here than usual. Tonight is no exception. He's s-sound asleep."

"Come back inside before you catch cold." His warm breath stirred her hair and made clouds of vapor in the frigid night. "You don't want to get sick and pass it on to Brady."

He had her there. She sighed. "All r-right."

When the hot air inside collided with her cold body, she really started to shiver.

"I'll pour you a glass of wine. That will help."

On the coffee table in front of the fireplace, beside the baby monitor, there was a bottle of red wine and two glasses. He filled them both a quarter full and handed one to her. Nudging the bottom, he urged her to sip.

She wasn't much of a drinker, but the ruby-colored liquid went down smoothly. "That's good."

"I'm glad you like it." He didn't sound glad. He sounded annoyed, if the clipped tone of his voice was any indication.

"Okay, then. I think I-I'll go up—" A sudden violent shiver stopped her words.

"Oh, for Pete's sake—"

Jason put her empty glass on the table, then turned her and rubbed her arms. The fire was to her front and he was at her back. Close. So very close. She was surrounded by heat and not in purgatory anymore. She felt the proof in every stroke of his hands on her arms. She wasn't on the outside looking in.

This was heaven.

Funny how the paradise oxygen supply was so doggone short.

"Are you warmer now?" He hadn't touched a drop of liquor, but there was a whiskey-and-chocolate huskiness in his voice that stole even more of her breath.

Was she warm? If the liquid heat pooling inside her was anything to go by, her body temperature had shot up past normal as soon as he touched her.

"Y-Yeah. I'm fine."

"That makes one of us." His hands stopped moving and he squeezed her arms, gently drawing her against the solid length of his body.

"You're not fine? What's wrong, Jason?"

He turned her and stared down. A frown, dark and intense, made his expression forbidding. "Do you really not know how much I want you?"

How would she? What did she know about this sort of thing? All she knew was that she wanted him, too. She caught the corner of her lip between her teeth and saw his gaze settle on her mouth, his eyes darkening to the color of coal.

At the same time he lowered his mouth, his hands tightened on her arms and brought her to her tiptoes, to meet him. She braced for impact, but the touch was soft and gentle. The resulting firestorm inside her was anything but. Need tangled with the doubt, but it was no contest. Yearning, craving, longing swelled inside her and pushed out everything but this man.

She said against his mouth, "Do you really not know how much I want you?"

His hands tensed. "Are you sure? After this, there are no loopholes."

She couldn't think straight what with him playing her body

like a finely tuned violin. So the meaning didn't register. Right now she didn't care about anything, couldn't remember why this was a bad idea.

All she knew was that Jason was her husband. The one she'd saved herself for. Now, finally—*finally*—she would know the secret handshake. She would find out the mysteries and pleasures of being loved by a man.

She looked into his eyes and willed away the doubts. "I want this very much, Jason."

He dragged air into his lungs as he nodded. Then he took her hand and led her toward the stairs. Climbing them had never seemed to take so long, until now. But she'd waited far longer to give her virginity, and could manage a few more minutes. The hall light was on and trickled into the master bedroom.

Jason stopped beside the king-size, pine sleigh bed and turned to her. He cupped her face in his hands and kissed her deeply, then traced her lips with the tip of his tongue. Her mouth opened instinctively and he dipped inside, teasing, tasting, tempting.

Fire coiled in her belly, then spread outward and grew until she thought her insides would implode. His hands slid to her waist, then curved at her hips, drawing their lower bodies close. She knew the physical mechanics of sex and could feel that he seriously wanted her, which made her spirit soar.

He slid his palms up and beneath her sweater until his thumb brushed over the nipple on her left breast. It was as if Mother Nature had strung an electrical cord from that flash point to a place between her thighs. Her breasts ached for more as liquid heat pooled and settled between her thighs fueling the frantic need inside her.

"Oh, Jason," she whispered hoarsely. "I never—"

"Right there with you," he said, his own voice ragged and tight, as if his control was tenuous.

She'd done that to him. It was a heady feeling.

Jason took hold of the comforter and blanket, throwing both back in one powerful movement. Then he grabbed the hem of his flannel shirt and jerked it up and over his head, revealing the taut wedge of naked flesh and muscle just above the waistband of his jeans. Her palms itched to touch the contours of his chest and she lifted a hand without thinking.

When she hesitated, Jason smiled, a self-satisfied look that made her already pounding heart even more erratic. He gently took her wrist and settled her fingers on him, over his own hammering heart. Although she sensed his tension, he stood stone still while she explored the masculine expanse to her heart's content.

Sliding lower, she traced the skin just north of the button on his jeans and female satisfaction trickled through her when the touch made him draw in a quick breath.

"That's a dangerous game you're playing, Maggie."

She looked at his teasing expression. "I can handle it."

"Two can play," he warned, his voice a sexy growl that sent tingles dancing over her highly sensitized skin.

He took the hem of her sweater and tugged at the same time she lifted her arms to make it easier for him to undress her. Reaching behind her, he unhooked her bra and slid it down, letting it fall to the floor.

Maggie didn't have a chance to feel shy or embarrassed while he looked at her. Their eyes locked and his were as dark and mysterious as the sea during a storm. He pulled her into his arms and they were skin to skin from the waist up. Her bare breasts pressed into his chest and it was the most exquisite sensation she had ever known. He threaded his fingers in her hair and cupped the back of her head to hold her still for his kiss. As he thoroughly explored her mouth, the sound of his harsh breathing filled her, challenged her.

With an effort he pulled away and said, "I don't think I can wait, Maggie… It's been a long time for me. I don't know— if it's—" He shook his head.. "I'll make it up to you next time."

She had no idea what he meant. All she knew was the need consuming her was more than she could stand. And when he reached out to unfasten her jeans, his hand was shaking. She pushed it aside and unfastened her pants, then slid them down and stepped out of them. No man had ever seen her completely naked. For reasons not really clear to her the fact that he was her first time made her incredibly glad.

Nervous, but glad.

A satisfied look slid into his eyes as he let his gaze slide over her from head to toe. "You are absolutely perfect."

The words chased away any lingering nerves and she smiled. In the next instant he'd dropped his pants and let her see him. His erection was impressive and started the nerves buzzing inside her again. They threatened to immobilize her, but Jason took charge. He lifted her in his arms and settled her in the center of the big bed. The sheets were cold against her back until he slid in beside her and warmed her with his body.

He kissed her deeply, their mouths meshing until everything disappeared except the two of them and the amazing sensation of his strength enfolding her. Silky threads of pleasure snapped inside her when he cupped her breast in his hand. He lowered his head and took her nipple in his mouth, flicking it with his tongue until the tension inside her grew and her hips moved restlessly, her body instinctively asking for what she didn't understand she wanted.

Jason's hand glided over her abdomen and between her legs, nudging a finger inside her as if he understood what she needed. Her body took over and she bore down on his hand, needy and wanting as a moan slipped out from somewhere deep inside her. The sound was to his breathing what kerosene was to a campfire.

"I need you, Maggie," he said against her mouth. "Now—"

"Yes," she breathed. "Now…"

He shifted onto her, letting his forearms keep his weight from crushing her. "Wrap your legs around me," he urged.

She did as he asked and his hardness pushed against her. Then he probed gently into the tender folds of her femininity and felt him tense when he encountered resistance. He started to pull away and groaned when she tightened her legs around him.

He thrust again—harder—and the barrier gave way. There was a single sharp pain followed by the pleasurable sensation of him filling her. Suddenly his body went rigid and he groaned out his release.

But Maggie sensed tension still pumping through him and there was fury in the gaze he leveled at her. "Jason? What's wrong?"

"You didn't think it was important to tell me you're a virgin?"

Chapter Nine

Jason didn't wait for an answer to his question but rolled away and disappeared into the bathroom. When he came out wearing nothing but sweatpants, Maggie was standing by the bed wearing nothing but his flannel shirt. It covered her top but left most of her legs bare. Next to naked, it was the sexiest look he could imagine. Damned if his body wasn't telling him in the strongest possible terms that he wanted her again. How was that possible when he was so furious? With himself and with her.

Minutes ago he'd completely lost any kind of restraint where she was concerned, so he stopped before crossing the empty space between them. If he reached out and touched her again, it would be a test of willpower he wasn't sure he could pass.

"You had a boyfriend. Engaged to be engaged, you said." It came out as an accusation.

"I did." She rested one bare foot over the other looking so impossibly young and incredibly innocent that it was a mystery how he'd missed the signs. "But that's different from sex."

"Not these days," he snapped. "Was he gay?"

"Not unless I turned him," she said, her chin lifting defensively.

"He never touched you?" That was hard to believe. Almost from the first moment Jason had itched to explore the taste and texture of her.

"I didn't say that."

Unfortunately he wasn't angry enough to miss the wounded look in her eyes. And that was *his* fault. Nothing like reminding her the jerk hadn't wanted her. Clearly the boyfriend was an idiot who was too stupid to know what he'd passed up. And Jason was handling this with all the sensitivity of a demented water buffalo.

He planted his feet wide apart and crossed his arms over his bare chest because he wanted so badly to hold her. If he touched her again it would just make a bad situation really, really bad.

"What *are* you saying?" he asked.

That was a dumb question and not really the one he wanted to ask. Maybe because he didn't really want to know why she hadn't stopped *him* before he'd gone beyond the point of no return. She'd made it clear from the beginning that she didn't get attached because she cared too much. He'd used that as leverage to make the situation permanent. But he hadn't *married* her, married her.

Until tonight.

Before he'd lost the capacity for coherent thought he'd even had the presence of mind to warn her about closing the annulment loophole. It had slammed shut a little while ago. But that wasn't what bothered him most.

"Maggie, why didn't you tell me you'd never had sex?"

"I didn't think it was important information."

"Trust me, it's important," he said.

There was a flash of something in her eyes, something that said "I did it and I'm not sorry." "Not anymore."

"Yeah." He ran his fingers through his hair. "I was there."

He'd also been there for her throaty little moans. Those were the sounds that had sent him over the edge, on his way to a mind-blowing finish. The man who prided himself on being in charge, the guy who never met a problem he couldn't fix with money had lost control and taken her virginity.

There was no fix for that.

He'd known she was innocent—almost a nun. The memory of his father's words kept crashing against the inside of his skull. A novelty. If he'd known the whole truth of it, he'd have taken better care.

"Why is it important? Would it have changed anything?" she asked, taking a step forward.

"Yeah. I might have stopped."

She moved closer, right in front of him now. "Why?"

She was so innocent she couldn't even understand why her innocence was an issue. "Never mind. It's not important now."

"It's important to me." Her eyes pleaded. "What would you have done differently if you'd known that I'd never had sex before?"

It was like she knew just the right thing to say to get his juices flowing again. The exact right button to push to work him up. He'd just about managed to get his libido under control and she had to go and ask a question like that.

"You don't really want to know, Maggie."

"If that were true, I wouldn't have asked. I told you once that I didn't meet men because of my job and responsibilities. That doesn't mean I'm not curious. It's one of the reasons I left the convent."

"To have sex?" he asked, trying not to be shocked.

"Sort of."

"Maggie—"

"Don't get your boxers in a bunch." She held up a hand. "It wasn't that defined for me. I just knew there was a lot I hadn't experienced in life and never would if I took final vows. I was curious. Mother Superior advised me to leave, live and pray on the problem."

He couldn't believe he'd just had sex and now they were discussing convents and talking to God. If there'd ever been any doubt about where he'd end up in the hereafter, it was gone now.

He was going to hell for sure. "It doesn't happen often, but I don't know what to say to that."

She smiled. "You could tell me why you're so put out that I didn't tell you I'd never done that before."

Now that she'd moved closer, into the light, he could see the soft pink staining her cheeks. The shyness in her expression in spite of her straightforward questions. Maybe if he explained, she'd let it go and back off.

"Okay." He let out a long breath. "I would have gone slower. Made sure you were ready—"

"How?" Her expression was honest and open, curious. Cute as could be.

And she had no idea what this was doing to him. "I'd have touched you differently." Before she could ask, he added, "A woman's body has places that are extremely vulnerable and sensitive to touch."

"I see." She nodded.

He knew she didn't have a clue. Sexual pleasure was one of those things that pictures and words couldn't define. There was no substitute for hands-on experience.

And this conversation was killing him. Time to end it. "If I'd known, I would have been able to make it less uncomfortable for you."

"It wasn't that bad. And you said next time would be better."

For God's sake, he'd actually told her there would be a next time? Mental forehead smack here. He remembered now. But he'd meant that because it had been so long for him, he wouldn't be able to last. And he wasn't going there. In fact this conversation should have been over a long time ago.

He looked at the sliding-glass window that opened onto the balcony overlooking the lake. The glow of the outside light showed that the snow had stopped.

"The blizzard is over," he pointed out.

She glanced over her shoulder, then back at him. "That's a relief."

For him, too. "We're going home in the morning. Go get some sleep."

"But—"

He held up a hand. "I'm tired, and it will be a long day."

"You're still upset. We should talk."

"That's the last thing I want."

"I really don't get why you're so put out about this," she said. "Some men would be—I don't know—*pleased* that they were first. What is your problem?"

"Up until a little while ago, I didn't have one."

She frowned as her fingers toyed with one of the buttons on his shirt. "Jason, please—"

He swallowed hard at the sight of her in that shirt, remembering all too vividly what was underneath, how her soft skin had felt, how perfectly her curves fit his hands. "Please go, Maggie."

He walked over to the window and looked out, not really seeing anything. But the darkness outside reflected her watching him before she turned to leave.

Stopping in the doorway, she said, "I'm not sorry it happened."

That made one of them.

And this was a hell of a time to think about birth control. She was too innocent to be on the pill and he'd been completely unprepared for how much he'd wanted her. Surely fate wouldn't nail him for the lapse. It was once. One time.

Her next time *would* be better, but it wouldn't be him. The thought made him crazier than trying to explain sex to an ex-nun. When she was gone, he let out a long breath, but there was little relief in it.

He remembered telling her that she was best for his family and she'd asked what would happen if that changed. He hadn't answered because he didn't have an answer. Until now.

Sex changed everything. Virgin sex changed everything times ten. He just found out that she'd waited all this time to give herself to a man and made the mistake of letting that man be him. He was one selfish bastard and what he'd done made him feel even more responsible for her at a point when he was already pushing back against any emotional connection.

Emotional connections didn't last. It's why he'd hired her to keep things professional. Now he had proof that she was too good for him. On top of everything else, he was a liar. He wouldn't give her a second time.

No way was he going to further risk the life he'd so carefully choreographed for his son.

It was nearly nine o'clock when Maggie heard Jason's key in the penthouse door. Brady had gone to sleep over an hour ago and she was in her room, trying to read an article from a women's magazine on how to revitalize marital intimacy. One of the problems, and there were many, was that the information was based on a normal relationship. Nothing about her situation fell anywhere within normal limits.

She listened to the sound of his movements through the penthouse. First he checked on his son. Then she heard him in the kitchen and finally he went into his office to work. In the week since they'd returned from the mountains, the man had barely said two words to her. Maybe it was the fact that she spent so many hours of every day with an infant, but Maggie felt an overwhelming need for adult conversation.

This was new for her. Normally after six weeks she went on to a new situation and interacted with either a couple and their new infant, or a family needing an extra pair of hands during that first month and a half. Interaction was the key word.

After seven days and nights of the silent treatment from Jason Garrett, she'd had it. She slid off the bed and checked her hair in the mirror over the dresser. Brady was the sweetest baby in the whole world, but after twelve hours of feeding, burping, changing diapers, walking, bouncing, shushing and patting, she looked like something the cat yakked up.

The way Jason had been acting, she really shouldn't give a rat's behind about her appearance, but she did. She marched down the hall to see him, determined to have her adult conversation no matter what she looked like.

The door to his office was half-closed and she peeked inside, expecting to see him doing computer work. Her expectation couldn't be more wrong. He was sitting behind his desk, but that's as professional as he got. There was a bottle of whiskey in front of him and he was just tossing back the contents of a tumbler when he noticed her.

"Maggie."

She walked in and stopped in front of his desk. "You're not even working."

"Excuse me?"

"Jason, I need to talk to you."

"Is Brady all right? I just looked in on him and he was sound asleep. Did he—"

"He's fine."

"Then I don't understand—"

"That makes two of us."

His dark eyebrows drew together in a frown. "Is something wrong?"

Where did she start? "I need to talk to a grown-up. Someone who can articulate sounds of more than one syllable that actually make sense. Don't get me wrong. Brady is a sweet-heart. And I adore him. But he's not exactly a scintillating con-versationalist. I'm sure some day he'll be glib and charming. He's got the charm thing going for him already. But I really want to have a dialogue with someone who can talk back."

"I see." He glanced at the chairs in front of his desk. "Would you like to sit down for this dialogue? Or is it some-thing that needs to be said standing up?"

"No. Sitting is fine." She moved around the chair, then lowered herself into it.

They stared at each other for several moments and the corners of his mouth turned up. "Do you want to start?"

"Okay." Now that she was here, she didn't quite know what to say. Go for the cliché. "How was your day?"

"Besides the fact that there aren't enough hours in it?" He shrugged. "It was all right."

"Did you make a gazillion dollars and buy Brady a college of his very own?"

He laughed. "No. But I'm working toward a merger that will guarantee financial security for him and all his depen-dents ad infinitum."

"The deal with Nathaniel Gordon?"

He gripped the empty glass and slowly turned it. "Yes."

"How's that going?"

"Suffice it to say that the road to financial security is not without speed bumps."

"Even with friends?"

"Especially with friends," he confirmed.

"I'm sorry."

"Don't be." He met her gaze. "Tell me what Brady did today."

She tried to ignore the pang of hurt that he'd turned the thread of conversation to his son. After all, that's why she was here in his home. Except he'd made love to her. Remember-ing his lips kissing her everywhere, his hands touching her everywhere and the way he'd made her feel everywhere sent shivers through her. Since they'd returned home, he'd behaved like it never happened. If only she could do that.

This part needed to be said standing up, so she did, then put her hands on her hips as she stared down at him. "Why are you avoiding me?"

"I don't know what you mean."

"Oh, please." She pointed to his glass. "There might not be enough hours in the day, but you're not using all of them to secure Brady's future."

"I'm entitled to down time." There was a defensive edge to his voice.

"You call it down time. I call it hiding."

"What the hell are you talking about?"

"You're gone at the crack of dawn and home later every night. So late that you don't have to interact with me at all. Everything is different."

"I have a lot of work to do."

She looked pointedly at the whiskey bottle and empty tumbler on his desk. "I can see that."

"What's gotten into you?"

That was her point. "Jason, you've been steering clear of me since we made love."

There. She'd said it.

"You're imagining that." The words were automatic and the fact that he didn't quite meet her gaze was clear evidence that he didn't believe it any more than she did.

"I know caring for an infant isn't rocket science. Or multi-bazillion-dollar business. But I'm good at what I do. Well trained and intuitive. My intuition tells me that things are not the same between us since we got back from the cabin. If one is splitting hairs, everything turned upside down the night we were snowed in. I know it, and your actions since then prove it. Don't patronize me by denying it."

"I have the utmost respect for what you do. If I didn't, I wouldn't have married you."

Her very own personal lesson in the art of the deal. But the deal changed when he took her to his bed.

She sat down again on the edge of the chair. It was the perfect place since she was on an emotional edge.

"We were as close as a man and woman can be and I'd expected—" She gripped her hands together in her lap but refused to look away. "I'd hoped it meant we'd turned a corner in this relationship."

"There's no corner to turn."

"What does that mean?"

The tension in his expression was a lot like the one he wore during sex, but in all probability he wasn't finding pleasure this time. "Maggie, that night was a circumstance that I should have handled better. It's a biological fact that men have needs—"

"As do women." She remembered the need grinding through her while in his arms with the snow falling softly outside the window. It was magical and he was chalking it up to simple biology. "I had this talk with Sister Margaret when I was twelve." She glared at him and stood up again. "Just because I was still a virgin, doesn't mean I was raised on the moon."

"No one said you were."

"Then why are you acting as if I just fell off the rocket booster?"

He ran his fingers through his hair. "The truth is that I don't know how to act."

"If you'd tell me what's wrong, we could work on it together, like married couples should."

Now he stood. Agitation did that to a person and she ought to know. She'd never in her life been as agitated as she was now.

"That's the thing, Maggie. We're not a couple. Not really. What we have is a business arrangement."

The words shouldn't have hurt so much, but they did. "I

thought after that night—" She swallowed hard. "We made love, not business. That shifted everything. And it's not just a clash of testosterone and estrogen."

"This is exactly the reason I intended to keep things strictly business."

"Define *things*."

"You. Me. Brady—" A darkness slid into his eyes as he stared at her. "Sex complicates everything. It was my mistake, and I take full responsibility for what happened."

"Unfortunately you can't take it back, either."

"No." He blew out a breath. "I have been avoiding you. It's all I can do to try and go back to the way things were."

"You're kidding, right?" She did an internal head shake at the absurdity of the male thought process.

"I'm completely serious. The reality is that we have a business arrangement and it can never be more than that because my only concern must be my son. Emotional entanglements complicate a situation. Assumptions are made. People get hurt. I don't want to do that to you."

"So the reason you won't talk to me is all about me?"

"That's one way of putting it. For your sake I've been keeping to myself. I would never hurt you, Maggie. Brady needs you."

She hadn't realized how much she wanted him to say he needed her until he didn't. So much for not hurting her. It was an effort not to let him see how much he *was*. Way past time to shift the focus of this ill-advised conversation.

"Speaking of Brady, this situation isn't good for him."

"What do you mean?"

"By avoiding me, you're sacrificing time with him." Putting aside her bruised feelings, Maggie realized it was true. The tension between them was costing Brady his father. That was unacceptable. "I think you're right."

"I am?"

She nodded. "We have to go back to the way things were before. I know you have a company to run. But all your free time should be spent with your child. He has to be your priority. I'm completely fine with that."

He looked surprised. "Really?"

"Absolutely." She walked around the chair and stopped halfway to the door. "I'm glad we had this talk. To clear the air."

"Good. Me, too."

"So don't stay out too late tomorrow."

He saluted. "Yes, ma'am."

She couldn't manage a smile and concentrated on getting out of the room before any of the emotions swirling inside her slipped out. Her chest and throat felt tight from holding back. If only she could dislike him, but he was being noble. Hurtful, but noble. His motives were above reproach. It was all about Brady. She loved that baby, too, with all her heart. That was the only reason she would try and do the impossible. She would do her very best to pull off a miracle and go back to the way things were before making love with Jason.

That meant shutting off her feelings, and she just didn't know how to pull that off.

So much for her dialogue with someone who could talk back. She wished she could take back the conversation. Now that he'd spelled everything out, the air might be cleared, but the confusion? Not so much. And she hurt more than ever.

Chapter Ten

Jason parked his Lexus SUV in the medical building lot on Green Valley Parkway where the pediatrician had his office. He saw his car and driver in another space and knew Maggie was still here with the baby. One glance at the Rolex on his wrist told him the appointment time was a half hour ago. He'd hear about it; she was direct that way. A man always knew where he stood and what was on her mind.

Like when she'd said in no uncertain terms that avoiding her was costing him moments with his son. It had been a week since they'd cleared the air. Yeah. Right. If that were true, he wouldn't feel like he wanted to put his fist through a wall. Or explode. Or both.

He hurried through the lot and into the landscaped court-yard with medical offices on either side. Rocks were artfully arranged as a dry lake bed with water-smart plants in orange, yellow, purple and red scattered around for splashes of color.

After locating Dr. Steven Case's office, he walked into what felt like an alternate universe.

The waiting room was packed with women and small children. Some of the women with small children looked like they were children themselves. Or maybe he was older than he'd realized. This was Brady's four-month checkup. Jason had missed the two-month and Maggie had made her disapproval clear.

He tried to tell himself not repeating the mistake wasn't about that, but about being there for his son. Which was true. Her approval didn't matter to him one way or the other, and he almost believed that.

The office was done in shades of light green, blue and brown with textured paper on the walls. Generic upholstered chairs with wooden arms and legs interspersed with faux leather benches that lined the walls and, in the center of the room, formed a conversation area, although no one was actually conversing. He wasn't the only guy, but was definitely in the minority. This was primarily an XX chromosome zone. Some harried mothers were attempting to control toddlers whose patience had been tested to the limit. Others were doing their best to pacify infants who were not happy.

Had his mother ever sat with him in the pediatrician's office before she walked out on him forever?

The thought popped into his mind out of nowhere because he hadn't thought about her for a long time. His father had advised him not to waste energy on unimportant things and he'd believed that to be the case until being on his own with Brady showed him how important parenting was. Then Maggie walked through his front door and put a finer point on the lesson by showing him how important a mother was.

With some difficulty, Jason finally spotted Maggie in a corner with the baby. He walked over and sat beside her on the bench.

Maggie studied him. "Are you all right?"

Except for that mental hiccup a few moments ago he was great. "I'm fine."

"I was beginning to wonder if you were going to make it," she said.

"Has Brady been seen yet?"

"No."

"Then in doctor time I'm punctual."

She smiled. "He's glad you're here."

"Yeah. I can tell." He looked at his son, peacefully sleeping in the infant seat. "How come you're sitting all by yourself over here?"

"Haven't you ever heard that doctor's waiting rooms are a breeding ground for germs?"

"I guess I missed that breaking news."

"Well, it's true." She angled her head toward the most congested part of the waiting area by the receptionist's check-in window. "I'm trying to shield Brady from those mini microorganism makers over there. And I don't mean that in a good way. Granted, they're cute as can be, but they want to kiss him and touch him and we don't know where those hands have been."

He glanced over and nodded. "I would never have thought of that."

"That's what I'm here for."

That's what he kept telling himself. Brady needed her and to make sure he had her, Jason needed to keep *his* hands to himself. Not so easy when all he could think about was touching her again.

A door to the back office was opened by a young woman wearing blue scrub pants and a top with cartoon characters. "Brady Garrett?"

Maggie stood, a grim expression on her face. "Man your battle stations. We're up."

Jason lifted the car seat and followed her past the germ

section and into the inner sanctum where they were led to an exam room.

"Hi, I'm Lisa." She smiled. "Mrs. Garrett, if you'll get Brady undressed, I'll be back in a few moments to weigh and measure him."

"Okay."

When they were alone, Jason glanced at her grim expression and wondered if it was about being addressed as his wife, or disturbing Brady from a perfectly good nap. Or both. He liked hearing her called Mrs. Garrett.

She squatted down and undid the straps around the baby, then lifted him out. He squeaked and stretched and let out a whimper.

"He's not going to like this," she said. "I hope he pees all over the exam table."

"Retribution tactics. Is that really something you want to encourage?" he teased.

"When he's in therapy and the repressed memory surfaces after hypnosis, I'll take responsibility for the coping strategy. But you just wait until after he gets his shots. We'll talk again then."

"Shots? You didn't tell me there would be shots." He watched her undress the baby, who started to cry.

She cooed to the unhappy little guy. "I know, sweetie. I don't like this any more than you. I really hate to say this, but it's for your own good, pal."

"What about the shots?" Jason demanded.

"Immunizations. Four of them. One for every month of his little life. If I'd said anything, would you have shown up?"

"Of course."

"Well, I wish I didn't have to. We can put a man on the moon and build a space station in orbit. Wouldn't you think someone could figure out a way to immunize innocent babies in a noninvasive way?"

Before he could answer that, Lisa returned. "Okay, let's get his stats. If you'll put him on the baby scale, please."

Maggie picked Brady up and settled him on the contraption that, mercifully, had something to shield tender baby skin from the cold, unforgiving metal. Then the young woman measured his length and head circumference. In Brady's chart, she plugged the information into his growth graph.

"He's in the ninety-fifth percentile on everything."

Jason couldn't stop the grin. "An overachiever. That's my boy."

When Maggie cuddled his boy to her and the unhappy sounds instantly stopped, Lisa nodded. "Someone's getting pampered. Dr. Case will be in shortly."

As she was leaving, a tall man wearing blue scrubs walked in. "Hi, I'm Steve Case."

"We met in the hospital after Brady was born," he said, shaking hands. He'd seen no reason to explain the baby's biological mother wanted nothing to do with him. Jason had only talked with the doctor about the baby.

"I remember," the doctor said. "Hi, Maggie. How are you?"

"Good," she said.

She'd handled all the well-baby visits and had developed a rapport with the pediatrician. She was Brady's mother in every way that counted.

Dr. Case washed his hands at the sink, and while drying them with a paper towel, studied the notes on the chart. "His numbers look good. Let's see what's going on with Mr. Brady. If you'll put him on the exam table on his tummy."

Maggie did as directed and stood by protectively, her hand on his back. The baby immediately lifted his head and rolled to his back.

"Good job, buddy," the doctor said. "His weight and growth are right on the money. Do you have any concerns about his eating or sleeping patterns?"

"Yes," Maggie said. "When should I introduce solid food?"

When he pressed the stethoscope to Brady's chest, the

baby waved his hands, reaching for the long tube. "Just what I wanted to see." As he talked, he ran his hands over the baby—back, trunk and legs. After nodding with satisfaction, he looked at Maggie. "Keep doing what you're doing. We'll talk about cereal at his six-month visit. And vitamins. Let's let his system develop further before rocking the boat."

"Okay," she agreed. When the doctor removed the stethoscope, the baby started to cry and Maggie picked him up.

"My nurse made a note here that you might be holding Brady too much."

Maggie met his gaze. "I believe the term she used was *pamper,* but what she meant was *spoil.*"

"It's all right to let him cry sometimes," Dr. Case pointed out.

"Sometimes we do. But it's my—" she met Jason's gaze, but he figured she was doing fine "—it's our philosophy that when he cries, he's got a good reason. Figuring out what that reason is and reassuring him is the way to build trust. To make sure he knows that his needs will be met." She glanced around the room, her gaze settling on the scale. "This is an unfamiliar environment to him. He's stripped naked and cold. Then he's poked and prodded and feeling pretty vulnerable. In my opinion, he's got a good reason to express his dissatisfaction with the situation. And I *will* comfort him."

The doctor grinned. "Good for you."

Jason seconded that. Everything he'd done, all the frustration he felt in not touching her, was worth it when he thought about her not being there at all for Brady. That was unacceptable.

Dr. Case looked at both of them. "Next time we'll talk about what to expect in the coming months, including babyproofing Brady's environment."

"Okay," they said together.

"If you have any routine questions, we're here during office hours. For emergencies, one of four doctors in the group is on call, so don't hesitate. Brady is doing great. Keep up the good work. My nurse will be back in a minute." He shook hands again, then left the room.

Maggie looked up and said, "I really hate this next part."

"Way to make me feel better."

"You're a big boy. It's not you I'm concerned about—"

Before she could finish that thought, Lisa was back with several syringes on a metal tray. This time her look was sympathetic. "I know this is difficult. Do you want to hold him?"

"Yes," Maggie said without hesitation.

The nurse was good at her job and it was over quickly, but Jason was a wreck. If there was any way he could have taken the medicine instead, he'd have done it in a nanosecond. The first poke sent Brady into a fit of hysterical crying. Maggie cuddled and comforted the baby and didn't seem to notice that he peed on her instead of the exam table.

"I know, sweetie. I'm so sorry. But it's going to be okay. I promise," she cooed against his cheek as he snuggled against her with absolute trust that his needs would be met. "Oh, my goodness, the tears."

Brady wasn't the only one. Jason saw the tears in her eyes, too, and his chest pulled tight.

"You're right," he said to her. "This part sucks."

For a man of action, this was a tough place to be. He wanted to comfort Brady, but his son wanted her and she was handling the situation better than he ever could. She was strong and sexy at the same time and it blew him away. Her bottomless capacity for caring made her as beautiful on the inside as she was on the outside. He shouldn't be thinking about any of that at a time like this, but he could because Brady wanted her, not him.

He'd bought his son a mother but making Maggie his wife in every sense of the word was a step he couldn't take. It would make everything personal and destroy the stability he was striving to provide his son. A stability he'd never known in his own life.

If he hadn't slipped up and made love to her, maybe this problem would be easier. But he *had* slipped up and made everything more difficult.

He'd tasted her intoxicating innocence and knew how sweet it felt to have her in his arms. Resisting her now was his hell to pay, because resist her he must.

Somehow.

Maggie felt like roadkill.

Her head hurt. Her throat was raw. And if there was any part of her body that didn't ache, she wasn't aware of it. The tightness in her chest made it hard to breathe, although that was much improved since her visit to Mercy Medical Center's E.R. She'd rather die than give what she had to the baby, so keeping to herself in her room was the only solution. In bed propped up with pillows, she was trying to work up enough oomph to look at the book on her nightstand even though reading it would take more energy than she could rally.

Jason peeked in her half-open door. "You're awake."

"What was your first clue?" Her voice was hoarse.

"Your eyes are open and you're sitting up. That's an improvement."

"If you say so."

He walked over to the bed and put his hand on her forehead. "How do you feel?"

"Go away." She shrank away from him and put her palm over her nose and mouth. "I'm contagious."

"I've already been exposed."

"Maybe. But now you're tempting fate. I'm in quarantine."

"A maxi-microorganism maker?"

"Yes. And if I taught you anything it's to stay away from people like me."

"Because the strategy worked so well for you," he said wryly. "Obviously you caught this at the pediatrician's office."

She'd already guessed that. "Is Brady sick?"

"No. He's fine."

"So the strategy worked. I'm probably run down." Brady had been up a lot at night. Probably teething. She hadn't had a lot of sleep lately. "The microorganisms found a fertile environment and invited all their friends to the party."

"They must have been having a good time judging by how sick you are."

She ducked out of range when he reached his hand out again. "Go away. It's not just your health I'm concerned about. I'm out of commission, and Ginger couldn't send anyone over on such short notice. Brady needs you to be in tip-top shape."

"I'll take the risk."

He was so lying. If he was really a risk taker, he'd have agreed to open up about why he'd pulled back from her. He'd have agreed to work on making what they had a marriage instead of a business arrangement. When she glanced up he was staring at her, intensity tightening his features. Had she said all that out loud? Her head felt as if it was filled with cotton so thinking straight was a challenge.

The mattress dipped from his weight when he sat on the bed beside her. Their thighs nearly touched. This time she had nowhere to go and his cool palm settled on her hot forehead. The sensation was so heavenly, she couldn't quite hold in a sigh.

"How do you feel?" he asked.

"You tell me."

"I think you still have a fever. In the E.R. they clocked you at a hundred and two."

"I still say it wasn't necessary to take me to Mercy Medical Center."

"Breathing shouldn't be that difficult. I made an executive decision." He brushed his knuckles over her cheek. "For the record, the doctor agrees with me."

"Executive decisions are what executives do."

"Speaking of executives, Mitch Tenney—"

"Who?" she croaked.

"The doctor in the E.R. at Mercy Medical. His name is Mitch Tenney. His wife is a behavior-modification coach who works with executives on strategies to resolve conflict in the work place."

"Oh?" She didn't feel much like talking or listening, but she liked having him there and that response took the least amount of effort to encourage conversation.

"Yeah. I've been thinking about instituting a corporate program like that, and he had some interesting information. It seems that not long ago he was encouraged to get counseling. That's how he met his wife—Samantha Ryan. Her father is the administrator at Mercy Medical."

"I see." When her nose started to run, she grabbed a tissue from the box next to her and mopped up. Part of her wanted him to go away and leave her alone to look like the wrath of God. The part that wasn't sick wanted him to stay forever.

"They're expecting a baby—Sam and Mitch."

"I didn't realize the E.R. was the hottest place in town for a male-bonding experience."

He had the audacity to grin. "We bonded over Brady. The doctor was quite taken with him since he'll be a father soon. And I met Dr. Cal Westen, an E.R. pediatrician. He's the guy in the group who doesn't see anyone in the Mercy Medical E.R. over eighteen. I'm told that kids are not just small adults and need doctors who understand that."

"I hope Brady never needs them, but it's good to know they're there."

"I got a lot of information while waiting for you."

"I'm sorry it was so long. You should have taken Brady home."

"And left you there?"

"I could have called a cab," she said.

"Transportation wasn't my biggest concern at the time." His grin disappeared and a worried frown took its place. "You had to have several breathing treatments to open up your airways."

"Apparently you and Dr. Tenney bonded over medical stuff, too."

"You had an asthma attack, Maggie."

"Thanks for the newsflash." She pulled at the tissue still in her hands.

"Have you ever had one before?"

"Yeah. But not—" She started coughing. At least it wasn't the tight sound of an asthmatic cough. It was deep and chesty and flulike.

"Damn it." Jason stood and left the room.

For Brady's sake it really was for the best that he keep his distance, although she instantly missed him. It was sweet that he actually seemed concerned about her. Genuinely worried that she was okay. She sighed again.

How stupid was she? Jason Garrett was a decent guy. If there was one thing she knew about him it was that he tried to do the right thing. His instincts registered in the noble range on the humanity scale. His recent attention was not evidence that his feelings had changed. It probably meant only that he didn't want her to stop breathing on his watch. And she was pathetic for even allowing the thought to enter her mind that it could be anything more.

She closed her eyes when she felt a pain in her chest, not entirely sure it had very much to do with the flu.

"Maggie?"

Jason's voice was a whisper, but it got her attention and she looked at him. He was standing beside the bed with a glass in his hand. There was a flex straw in the liquid.

He held it out. "Drink this."

"I'm not thirsty."

"Mitch said you need to hydrate. That means lots of fluids."

"I know what it means. You tend to hear it a lot when you have asthma attacks on a regular basis."

"You do?"

"Not anymore. Not since I was about sixteen or seventeen. I think as I grew my lungs got bigger and it allowed me to compensate. But when I was having the attacks, it was long enough."

"For what?"

"To keep me from being adopted." She met his gaze and saw the pity there. "Good Shepherd encourages families in the community to take in kids. They work with one of the local TV stations, do pictures on the Internet and everything possible to find permanent homes for the kids. It's not that no one wanted me—"

"But?"

Apparently her thoughts had taken a turn for the pathetic. She wished she could take back the words, but now that she'd told him, he wasn't likely to let it pass. "I had a medical problem that adoptive parents just didn't want to take on. So that's why Good Shepherd was my permanent home until I was eighteen."

He set the glass on the nightstand and settled beside her on the bed. "I'm sorry, Maggie."

"You have nothing to be sorry for." Well, maybe he should be sorry he couldn't love her. Her weakened condition was the only excuse for letting that thought form.

"It's a lousy thing to go through."

"What doesn't kill you makes you stronger." She shrugged.

The cliché was meant to be spunky speak but it must have come out pretty high on the pity scale because he maneuvered himself beside her and slid his arm behind her back, pulling her against him as he leaned against the piled-up pillows.

She should have protested that proximity to her was dangerous because she was highly contagious. She could have

believed that her weakened condition made resistance too
much effort. The truth was that his shoulder was nice to lean
an aching head against. Having his arms around her simply
felt too wonderful. Staying put meant letting down her guard,
but the reward was so worth the risk.

She sighed and let her eyes drift shut. For just a little while
she didn't have to put up a brave front and be strong. She could
leave it all to Jason. The concept of not being completely on
her own was incredibly appealing and she could be forgiven
for wanting it to go on forever. It was a perfectly normal
reaction to wish things were different. That *she* was different,
the type of woman he could be attracted to.

Her eyes drifted closed as the fuzziness in her head took
over. "If only I was someone you could love even though your
father doesn't want you to," she whispered.

Had she said that out loud?

Of course not. She wouldn't do that. It was just the flu
talking, making her head fuzzy. She felt like roadkill, but if
there was a silver lining, it was that finally she was in bed with
her husband.

Chapter Eleven

"Jason, you must have better things to do than come with me to Good Shepherd."

In the penthouse foyer, he picked up the baby in his car seat, then slung the diaper bag over his shoulder. "Not really."

"It's not that exciting. Lots of kids. Making meals. Doing crafts." She shrugged. "You'll probably be bored out of your mind."

"It's my mind." He smiled. "Boring sounds nice after all the excitement recently."

It had taken almost a week, but he noticed the shadows beneath her big blue eyes were finally fading and there was a little color in her cheeks. The well-worn jeans and Good Shepherd T-shirt tucked into the loose waistband showed that she'd lost weight during her illness. Definitely too much excitement. He liked order and stability and that didn't happen when Maggie wasn't in tip-top form. He wanted her strong and sassy and in his face about whatever was her current peeve.

When she tilted her head to the side, her dark, silky pony-tail brushed her thin shoulder. "But after a long work week, I thought you enjoyed time alone with Brady."

"We had lots of bonding time when you were sick."

And that was the reason he wasn't letting her do the volunteer shift by herself. A relapse wasn't happening on his watch. She hadn't been out of bed that long and he intended to make sure she didn't push herself too hard. He didn't ever want to be as scared as when he'd watched her struggle to draw air into her lungs. And she didn't know it yet, but she wasn't staying overnight.

"You're sure about this?" she asked.

"I've never been more sure of anything."

"Okay." Her tone filled in the part about it being his funeral.

He drove them in the Lexus with Maggie in the front passenger seat and Brady in the rear. This was the first time the three of them had gone anywhere without a driver. It felt so amazingly—normal. Father, son and…mother? Something shifted inside him and he wasn't at all comfortable with it.

Using Maggie as his GPS, Jason followed her instructions and within fifteen minutes they pulled up in front of the old Victorian with the sign out front that proclaimed Good Shepherd Home for Children. After exiting the SUV with the baby and his stuff, they waited on the porch after ringing the bell.

An older woman answered. "Maggie!"

Maggie hugged her. "Hi, Sister Margaret."

This was the woman who'd found her as an infant on this very porch. Jason wasn't sure what he'd expected, maybe wings and a halo. To him the nun looked pretty ordinary in her faded-black slacks, pink-, purple-and-white striped cotton blouse. Her hair was short, gray-streaked brown and her eyes pale blue.

When Maggie pulled out of the hug, she glanced at him and held out a hand indicating the baby, asleep in his car seat.

"That is Brady Hunter Garrett and this is his father. Jason, this is Sister Margaret Connelly."

He held out his hand. "It's a pleasure to meet you, Sister."

"Likewise." When she put her fingers in his the effects of hard work were evident.

She smiled approvingly at him. "Mr. Garrett, I don't know what Maggie said to prompt your generosity toward Good Shepherd, but I can't thank you enough. If not for you, the home would probably have been shut down by now."

"I'm glad I could help."

He glanced at Maggie. Since she was putting a lot of effort into avoiding his gaze after *not* introducing him as her husband, the look on her face could only be guilt. Obviously, she hadn't broadcast the news of their marriage to Sister Margaret. The details were something he didn't talk about, either, but he wasn't a snap to read. Maggie must have been one of the easy ones to raise. If she ever tried to pull a fast one, the evidence would be right there in her eyes. Innate honesty was just one more thing about her to like.

"Let me show you what we've been able to do with your donation," Sister Margaret said.

"I'm not here for an accounting of the funds," he assured her.

Sister laughed. "I didn't think you were. But it would mean a lot to me for you to see that the money has been well spent."

"All right then."

"I'll just go see the kids," Maggie said.

"Come with us, Maggie," Sister protested. "The older ones just started watching a movie. The little ones are napping. And I know you've been sick. Don't wear yourself out."

Jason liked the way this woman thought. "That's what I've been trying to tell her."

"Follow me," Sister said.

As she hurried ahead, Jason leaned down so only Maggie

could hear. "Someone's been fibbing to the nun. Is that like lying to God?"

"I didn't tell an untruth to anyone." Her eyes flashed indignantly.

"At the very least it's a lie of omission to conceal the fact that we're married."

The flash disappeared from her eyes, replaced by something that made him wish for indignance. "You can't have it both ways, Jason."

"What does that mean?"

"Being married when it suits you and not thinking about it the rest of the time." The baby picked that moment to wake up and cry. "We both know we're married in name only."

Except for that one time at the cabin a couple weeks ago. And she couldn't be more wrong. He thought about it a lot, then took a cold shower whenever possible.

Sister Margaret walked back to them and looked sympathetically at the crying infant. "I didn't mean to lose you. I'm so used to hurrying. There's always something waiting to be done."

"If it's all right with you, Sister, I'll stay here and feed Brady."

"Of course, dear." She looked up at him. "This way, Mr. Garrett."

"Jason, please."

"All right."

After taking him through the bathrooms and kitchen to proudly show off the new plumbing fixtures and appliances, she led him outside and pointed out the brand-new roof, red tiles that contrasted with the beige stucco and stood out against the clear blue sky. The house was situated on at least an acre of property in the older section of Henderson. There was a playground with swings, jungle gym and other pieces of equipment set up on the more forgiving rubberized ground instead of blacktop.

For the older kids there was a basketball court, volleyball nets and baseball backstop.

"This is quite a place you have, Sister."

"I wish there was no need for a home like this," she said. "Unfortunately Las Vegas needs even more. It bothers me that I can't help all the children who are disadvantaged and deprived."

"I'm glad you were here for Maggie." He hadn't meant to say so, no matter that it was true.

"I remember the night Sister Mary and I found her. It was freezing outside." She shook her head. "She was so tiny, and so quiet. She never cried. It's a miracle we found her out there. If we hadn't…"

He was glad she didn't finish the thought. It wasn't something he wanted to hear because he couldn't imagine a world without Maggie's sweetness in it. "She told me that her asthma kept her from being adopted."

"It's true. A couple came very close to taking her once, but money and medical insurance were an issue. After it didn't work out Maggie asked why they couldn't love her. The children can't understand financial or other considerations, so they personalize everything." Sister looked up. "It was a conversation that broke my heart. Maggie is very special and very easy to love."

The words and look made him squirm because he didn't believe in a love that would last forever. The only kind he understood was what he felt for Brady.

He glanced over his shoulder at the house. "We should find Maggie. See if she needs a break from the baby."

They walked back inside and went to the kitchen where Maggie was sitting on one of the long benches. An empty bottle of formula was on the wooden table beside her and she had Brady over her shoulder, patting his back to burp him.

"Hi. What do you think of the place?" she asked him.

"Very nice."

Sister looked proud. "Because of your help with the

building contractors, Jason, we had enough money left over from the absolutely necessary repairs to have the inside painted and start a scholarship fund."

"I'm glad to hear that." He made a mental note to pad that scholarship fund a little more. He looked down at Maggie and said, "You look tired. Let me take Brady."

"Okay." She kissed the boy's cheek before handing him up.

"Hey, buddy," Jason said, putting Brady over his shoulder. The boy let out a big belch and he laughed. "He begs your pardon, Sister, but it's a sound that does a father proud."

Sister smiled as she gazed at them. "You work well together. Like a regular family."

"In a way," he said, glancing at Maggie. He wasn't going to rat her out and tell Sister the terms of their agreement. "But we're not very traditional."

"Neither is this home, but we're a family nonetheless." Sister shrugged. "You can't change the hand you're dealt, but it's how you play the game that makes the difference. Family is what you make for yourself."

"Or don't make," he said, because he chose not to play at all.

Sister leaned a hip against the table as she frowned up at him. "Why would you do that? Why would you choose not to be part of a family?"

"It's safer." He and Maggie both understood that.

"Then you're shortchanging yourself." She took them both in with a look that suggested she could read minds. "The Bible teaches that faith, hope and love are virtues. And the greatest of these is love."

"If it's the greatest," he said, "then love has the most potential for pain."

"You're very cynical, Jason." She folded her arms over her chest. "What—or should I say who—made you that way?"

"My father," he answered. If anyone but Sister Margaret had asked, he would have shut them down. But she was a nun.

"Other than Brady, he's my only family. Whatever virtues I have—or don't have—are because of him."

And that's why he needed Maggie. His father had hammered home the fact that loving someone was the first step to losing them. He'd been raised on cynicism. She was sweetness and light to his darker side. Optimistic to his pessimistic. Loving to counterbalance his deliberate detachment. It was the only way he knew how to be and it wasn't good enough anymore because he wanted better for Brady.

Mental backspace and delete. Correction: his son needed Maggie. Jason wouldn't let himself need her or anyone else again.

Late at night when she tiptoed into the kitchen, Maggie noticed the dim light beneath the microwave was on. Jason must have forgotten to turn it off. She filled a mug with water and set it inside the appliance to heat. Maybe a cup of chamomile tea would help her to sleep.

"Is something wrong, Maggie?"

Heart pounding, she whirled at the unexpected sound of his voice. Jason was sitting at the dinette, which was shrouded in shadow.

"Good grief, you startled me." She pressed a hand to her chest. "I didn't see you there."

"Are you all right? Is Brady settled?"

"He's fine. I got him back to sleep a few minutes ago. I think he might be teething." While the microwave hummed beside her, she leaned against the counter.

"You think? Aren't you the baby expert?"

"Aside from the fact that babies are unpredictable and can't talk to tell us what's wrong," she said. "My area of expertise is birth to six weeks. After that I move on."

"Until I convinced you to stay," he said.

"Yes." They both knew why she was here and she didn't

want to talk about it. "What are you doing up? Did Brady's crying wake you? I tried to soothe him quietly but he—"

"It wasn't that." He lifted a small glass to his mouth and three guesses said it wasn't chamomile tea. "And thanks for taking care of him. Technically this is your night off."

But Brady had long ago stopped being a job. She loved him, and he'd needed her to comfort him. It was probably a good thing she'd let herself be talked out of staying at Good Shepherd.

"It was pretty underhanded of you to get Sister Margaret on your side. Two against one was not a fair way to keep me from staying the night as usual."

"You're stubborn and I needed a good wingman. Or nun," he said.

She laughed. "Sister Margaret would like that. The 'wing-nun.'"

"She's pretty cool. You were lucky to have her growing up."

"I know."

"She's got good instincts, and I think you picked up on that while you were at Good Shepherd."

Something in his voice bothered Maggie. The sandpaper edges were ragged and she didn't think it was about Brady teething.

She took her warm water from the microwave, put her teabag in it, then joined him at the table. The shadows in this corner were her friend since she was wearing an old Runnin' Rebels T-shirt with no bra underneath and a pair of plaid cotton pajama bottoms. The fashion police could just suck it up.

Jason wasn't dressed for bed, unless he slept in worn jeans and a long-sleeved white cotton shirt. With his long legs stretched out and crossed at the ankles, she noticed his feet were bare and wondered why she found that so incredibly intimate. And worse, so amazingly arousing.

She pulled out a chair at a right angle to him and sat. "What's wrong, Jason?"

He looked at her and a spark of amusement had his mouth curving up at the corners. "Aren't we Miss No-Nonsense tonight?"

"Like you said, I've learned from the best. Sister Margaret is the queen of no-nonsense. So don't try to change the subject. Something's bothering you or you'd be asleep."

He stared at her for so long it appeared he wasn't going to answer. Finally, he sighed. "It was something Sister said about the three virtues."

"I remember. The greatest of these is love." She met his gaze. "And when you said love provides the greatest potential for pain, I saw the look on your face."

"What look?" He didn't move, but the tension rolling off him was almost palpable. "What did you see?"

"That someone had hurt you badly. Who was it, Jason?"

"Do I have to pick?"

He was trying to make light of it, but she refused to be sidetracked. At least not without a fight. She had him on the ropes. Now was the time to ask what she most wanted to know. The question he was least likely to answer. "Have you ever been in love?"

"Yes."

For some reason that surprised her. Not just that he responded, but because he admitted he'd cared deeply. She knew he was capable. His deep feelings for Brady were proof. But caring for a woman seemed unexpected. "Who?"

"April Petersen."

She waited but more details were not forthcoming. He was going to make her work for it. "When?"

"My first year of college. I was almost nineteen."

By now she knew the only way she'd get this story was question by question. "What happened?"

"Why did something have to happen? Couldn't it just not have worked out?"

She shook her head. "That's not what the look on your face said. Definitely something went down and it wasn't happy."

"There was a third party involved."

"She cheated on you?" Maggie asked, outraged for him. He was Jason Garrett. Who in their right mind would jeopardize love and a beautiful future with him?

"No." He smiled, but there was no humor in it. "At least not that I know of."

"Then I don't understand. Why didn't it work out?"

"Because my father paid her a great deal of money to disappear from my life."

She blinked at him, waiting for the "gotcha." When he stared back, misery in his eyes, she knew he wasn't kidding. "That's just nuts," she said.

For the first time since joining him, a genuine smile touched his lips. "I'll be sure to tell Hunter you said that."

"I'd welcome the opportunity to ask him what the heck he was thinking."

"Heck?" One dark eyebrow rose. "I do believe that's a four-letter word coming from you."

"It's a four letter word, period," she scoffed. "And you're changing the subject. Why would your father do something like that? Couldn't he wait until the fire of young love burned itself out? That's what usually happens."

The guy she'd fallen for had proved that.

"My father found out that April and I were planning to elope."

"Okay." She nodded. "That's a little more serious and deserving of some fatherly intervention. But there's intervention and there's *intervention*. He couldn't have initiated a father-son dialogue to tell you it was a foolish, crazy idea?"

"That's not the way Hunter operates." He toyed with his glass. "He bought me friends, tutors and eventually admission to a college that supposedly had no openings. I learned that if you throw enough money at a problem, you can make it go away. And that's what he did with April."

Again she recalled his earlier words. Whatever virtues I have—or don't have—are because of him. Where was his mother? Too preoccupied by Jason's relationship with Brady's mother, Maggie couldn't remember if he'd ever mentioned the woman who'd brought him into the world. In for a penny, in for a pound. All he could do was tell her to mind her own business.

"What about your mother? Did she have any opinions on your elopement?"

"I wouldn't know. She left him when I was a kid."

Between the lines she heard that his mom left and didn't take him with her. But this was his mother. He must have some feelings about it but he didn't say more. A cold, unformed sort of dread seeped into her.

"Okay, so Hunter ran the show. But buying off your fiancée? Who does that?"

Irony was rife in the look he settled on her. "Isn't the better question—what kind of woman would go along with taking money to dump me?"

More coldness crept in. "She was young, too—"

"She swore to love me forever. She made declarations of unwavering faithfulness until my father put enough zeros on a check to get her attention. The next thing I knew she decided things wouldn't work out for us and walked away. Not long after, Hunter was only too happy to share the details."

Maggie rubbed her thumb on the handle of her mug. "Are you still in love with her?"

"April?"

"No. Barbarella," she teased. "Of course April."

He smiled. "No, I'm not still in love with her. And you're right. She was very young. So was I. That doesn't mean I wasn't ticked off at him for a very long time. And her." His hand tightened around the glass. "Anyway, to be honest, now that I have a son, I understand where my father was coming from."

"Where?"

"He was trying to prevent me from making a monumental mistake."

"Marriage is serious," she agreed. "But why did you feel the need to take that step? Why not just live together? I'm assuming you went away to college. You probably had a certain amount of freedom. Why take legal steps to make it permanent?" That time. As opposed to now with her and his need to ensure his son would have continuity of child care.

"Does it matter? That was a long time ago. She *was* young, but she couldn't cash that check fast enough. Obviously she never loved me as much as I—" He stopped, then tossed back the remainder of the liquid in his glass. "Forget it. I don't remember why I felt the need to get married." The look on his face said different. "Young and stupid. It's my story, and I'm sticking to it."

She nodded, knowing it was useless to push further no matter how much she wanted to understand why he kept her at a distance. "In general you're not especially chatty and in touch with your feminine side. That's more than I thought you'd say."

"Maybe I just knew resistance was futile because you learned from the best and I learned from…Hunter."

The cold feeling inside her chased away all the warmth. He'd learned from his father how to buy people off. In her case it was about securing permanent child care, but he'd paid for her services just the same. Clearly he didn't feel his father had been the best influence and didn't trust himself not to utilize the behavior he'd picked up in that environment. Who could blame Jason when his only role model was in financial negotiations with wife number four and already engaged to number five?

Jason refused to risk making the same mistakes and based

marriage on a business arrangement instead of emotions. He refused to open his heart, and that made her incredibly sad because she wanted very much for him to let her in.

Who would have guessed that an abandoned baby who grew up in an orphanage would be the lucky, well-adjusted one? He'd respected her instincts, but she wished for more worldly instincts that would help her heal his wounded soul. She hurt for his hurt and wanted to put her arms around him to take away his pain. She wished it were as easy and uncomplicated as soothing his son after immunizations.

But there was nothing simple and easy about the way she felt. With little or no effort she could fall head over heels in love with Jason Garrett.

And that was a problem, because he was right. If love is the greatest virtue, it *did* have the greatest potential for pain. Somehow, she had to stop feelings that were picking up momentum like a runaway train.

Chapter Twelve

Maggie listened intently to Savannah Cartwright, the Mommy & Me instructor at Nooks & Nannies, The Nanny Network Child Care and Learning Center. Sitting cross-legged on the floor with Brady in front of her, she smiled down at him and rubbed his belly as directed. "Does that feel good, big guy?"

Brady smiled and laughed, vigorously moving his arms and legs in response. He babbled happily and the sound was so joyful it was almost impossible for Maggie to be sad. Almost, but not quite. It was hard learning to coexist with a man who made it clear he would never be part of a couple. A man she couldn't stop thinking about with his shirt, and everything else, off.

She'd tried to keep him out of her heart and then he'd been so sweet and solicitous when she was sick. Were those the actions of a man who didn't care? But then she'd found out that love had kicked him in the teeth. No wonder he wanted no part of it again.

Petite, blond and twentysomething, Savannah squatted on

the rug beside her, smiling down at Brady. "You're a happy fella, aren't you?"

His arms and legs stilled while he stuffed a chubby fist in his mouth, intently studying the stranger.

The instructor looked around at the other women interacting with their children and said, "Brady is responding appropriately to his environment and the situation. I'm unfamiliar. He's communicating that by ceasing the happy, carefree movements of moments ago. When he gets to know me, he'll smile with pleasure at a recognizable face, just like the rest of the babies who have been coming for a while."

There were eight in the class, sixteen if you counted the babies. Maggie's new normal was trying to get back her presex mentality toward Jason. Now she knew more about his trust issues and that she needed to focus all her energy on growing Brady instead of growing a relationship with his father. She'd joined the class that morning and didn't feel the need for full public disclosure about the fact that she wasn't Brady's biological mother.

Savannah smiled at the baby, then continued coaching the group. "Remember, tummy time is about developing your baby's interest in the world through sensory perception. Just like the massage techniques we practiced earlier it's about giving your baby generous amounts of attention to make him or her feel comfortable, safe and secure. All the skills these babies are developing by turning toward sounds, looking at and tracking interesting sights facilitates learning and helps them connect with loved ones."

Like the other women there, Maggie rubbed, gently scratched, tickled and touched Brady's tummy, making him laugh as he rolled from side to side. She watched carefully for all the signs that he'd had enough and when the reactions to stimulation were less enthusiastic, she picked him up and cuddled him to her.

Savannah nodded approvingly. "Way to go, Maggie. Reading your baby is important. When the current activity is not energizing the child, it's time to stop. Too much of a good thing and all that."

Pride might be a sin, but Maggie couldn't help being pleased with herself. She'd never cared for a baby into this stage of life and to know her instincts were on target made her feel good. She remembered what Jason had said about getting her good intuition from Sister Margaret while growing up at Good Shepherd. The stab of unhappiness at remembering that conversation with him made her realize again how many memories she was making that would have him as the star.

Savannah looked at the clock on the wall, then at everyone on the floor. "Time is up for today, ladies. I'll look forward to seeing you all here next week."

Maggie settled Brady on the portable pad she'd brought and changed his diaper, then gathered all her things while the other women moved off to the side to chat. She felt like an outsider, and not just because she was the new kid on the block. To make friends she'd have to share part of herself and she just couldn't.

She walked out of the room and down the hall, on her way to the parking lot where the driver and car waited. As she passed an office, someone called to her. She poked her head in the room and saw Ginger Davis. An attractive woman with short blond hair sat in a visitor chair in front of her desk.

"Hi, Maggie."

Ginger had to be right around fifty, but hardly looked a day over thirty-nine. Her brown hair fell in layers to her shoulders and was fashionably highlighted.

She smiled at her former boss. "Ginger. I didn't know you'd be here."

"I had a meeting and here at the learning center was the most convenient place for it." She looked at the woman. "This is Casey Thomas. Casey, meet Maggie Shepherd. She used to work for The Nanny Network, until receiving an offer she couldn't refuse. She recently got married."

Casey smiled. "Congratulations."

"Thanks," Maggie answered, feeling like a fraud for impersonating a happily married woman.

"Casey came in for her yearly evaluation. She's retired from the military. The army's loss is The Nanny Network's gain."

"Wow," Maggie said. "Taking care of kids is really a big change for you."

Casey nodded. "In a good way."

"Don't let me interrupt you," Maggie said.

"I was just leaving." Casey stood and looked at Ginger. "Thanks for understanding where I'm coming from."

Her ex-boss nodded. "It's exactly what I need to know to match you with the right client. I appreciate your time and honesty, Casey."

"No problem." She passed Maggie in the doorway. "Nice to meet you."

"Same here."

When they were alone, Maggie walked into the office. Ginger stood and moved from behind the desk, resting a hip on the corner. In her olive-green crepe pantsuit and low-heeled pumps, she looked every inch the business woman, attractive and successful. But Maggie had heard bits and pieces of her personal history, not the complete background check the woman did on prospective employees, but enough to know her past hadn't been speed-bump free.

"Maggie, what are you doing here?"

"I brought Brady to the—" She hesitated, feeling weird even saying it.

"Mommy & Me?" Ginger asked.

"Yes." She sat in the visitor chair Casey had just vacated.

Ginger looked down at the baby in the car seat who was studying her with dark eyes very much like his father's. A wistful, painful expression flashed across her face, then disappeared. "He is an absolutely adorable baby."

"You'll get no argument from me." Again she remembered Jason saying the same thing.

"So, how's married life?"

Maggie smiled as widely as possible and it made her cheeks hurt. "Fantastic. Could not be more wonderful."

"And Jason?"

"He's pretty amazing."

At least that part wasn't a lie. The man was honorable, caring, handsome, sexy and out of reach. The fact that he'd married someone like her was pretty amazing. And then there was the sex....

"Really?" Ginger's brown eyes seemed to burrow inside her, as if she could see all that festered there. "You know, we never did have a chance to discuss your situation. It was all so sudden. Was it love at first sight?"

"Something like that."

"Is this fantastic, couldn't-be-more-wonderful marriage everything you thought it would be?"

"And more." And less, Maggie admitted only to herself.

Ginger shook her head, a clear indication she wasn't buying the act. "What's wrong? There's something you're not telling me."

Maggie sighed and shook her head. "Am I that easy to read?"

"What's going on?" Ginger asked.

"I was determined to leave Jason's after six weeks. I even told him the sad story of why my terms are in place. He ignored it all and proposed marriage, security for all of us. In exchange, he agreed to give the Good Shepherd Home the money to make the necessary building repairs so they could pass the state inspection."

"Oh, Maggie—" Ginger frowned. "He paid you money to marry him?"

"It sounds weird and cheap when you say it like that. But essentially—yes."

"What are your expectations from this marriage?"

"It would be easier if you asked what they were when I agreed to it."

"Okay." Ginger folded her arms over her chest. "Start there."

"All I could think about was Good Shepherd closing and what would happen to the kids. The system is already over-crowded and they'd have nowhere to go. I love that place," she said simply. "I had to do something and Jason gave me a solution. On top of that, I wanted to stay with Brady. Selfish, I admit, but true." She looked down at the now-sleeping infant and smiled tenderly. "Beyond that I wasn't thinking."

"That's obvious." Ginger studied her. "Also obvious is that you don't look happy."

"I'm just tired." More than usual, actually, which she couldn't entirely explain away by chalking it up to the energy drain of caring for an infant.

"This is me and I'm not buying that. There's more you're not saying." Ginger shook her head. "I can't believe this. I feel so responsible."

"But why?"

"I sent you to him. He had a crisis situation and you're the best under those circumstances. It never occurred to me that he'd make an indecent proposal."

"It wasn't indecent. He's the most decent man I've ever met. He's—"

"What?"

How did she answer that? How could she put into words what he was like now that she'd experienced the amazingness of being in his arms, of joining in the most personal way? She knew the incredible, profound bond a man and woman could share and it was magical. But she wanted more magic. She wanted him.

Ginger watched intently when she said, "Tell me, Maggie, do you want a real relationship with Jason?"

For one perfect evening she'd had it all, everything she'd ever yearned for. Remembering made her response simple. "A marriage in every sense of the word is exactly what I want."

"All right then." Ginger tapped her lip. "You need to let him know."

"I already tried that. We had a talk and he doesn't feel the same. He's pretty damaged from some stuff in his past."

"I knew his mother. And I've met his father. I can see where he'd have 'stuff.'" Ginger's expression was grim. "But really, Maggie, has your life been a fairy tale?"

"Of course not."

"Mine, either. But you have to move on and if there's an opportunity for happiness, you reach out and grab it or life passes you by." Ginger took a breath. "We're all damaged in one way or another. Get over it."

"So what are you saying?" Maggie asked.

"You have to fight for him."

"I told you, I already did—"

"That was conversation. I'm talking about fighting dirty."

Maggie blinked. "I don't know what you mean. Dirty? I'm not sure—"

"I'm saying use every weapon in your female arsenal. Candles. Wine. Lingerie."

"Seduce him?" Maggie blushed.

Ginger grinned. "That's the spirit."

She was being advised to seduce her husband, something Maggie couldn't imagine Sister Margaret telling her to do. Yet it didn't feel wrong. Jason had wanted her once or he wouldn't have taken her to his bed. The intense expression he wore ever since was identical to the way he'd looked that night. If it was anything to go by, he still wanted her.

What was wrong with helping the situation along?

* * *

In the nursery glider chair, Jason moved slowly back and forth with his almost-asleep son cradled against him. A chubby little hand rested over his heart. The sight tapped into a deep well of tenderness that sometimes threatened to swamp him. He would do anything for this child, give him anything he wanted even though he knew from personal experience that indulgence and interference weren't the preferred parenting style. That's why he was counting on Maggie. In the future when he agreed to some outrageous excess Brady requested, Maggie would remind him to initiate a father-son dialogue to tell him it was a foolish, crazy idea.

Brady stirred and sighed, his little fingers clutching Jason's shirt. The time he spent with his son in the evening was the best part of his day. Tonight was even more special because normally at bedtime the baby wanted Maggie.

Jason wanted her at bedtime, too, in a grown-up way. And every night he fought against it. Her recent illness had scared the crap out of him and he'd had to hold her, just to reassure himself she was okay. But feeling her soft skin and even softer curves in his arms had tested the hell out of his willpower and pushed him to the edge of resistance. If she hadn't been sick he wouldn't have been able to stop himself.

She was something else, he thought. Strong and straightforward. Like the night she'd confronted him about hiding from her. He still wasn't quite sure how she got him to admit she was right. The fact that his body told him he was ready for her made his declaration about wanting to go back to their pre-sex relationship all the more absurd.

It couldn't be more ironic that he'd had no trouble sleeping with women before he was married. Now that he'd tied the knot, sleeping with this particular woman was a major problem. His head was telling him hands off. His hands were in favor of ignoring his head. In fact, the majority of his physical components were rallying for sexual relief, which meant throwing out all the sensible and sane reasons for denying himself.

He rubbed Brady's back. "What's a dad to do, buddy?"

As the baby grew more limp in his arms, Jason figured it was time to see if he was deeply asleep. He stood and very gently set the boy on his back in the crib. Long, dark lashes fanned out just above his healthy round cheeks. After pulling up the blanket, he brushed the dark hair off Brady's forehead, then leaned down and kissed him.

"I love you, son."

The boy sighed in his sleep as if he'd heard and understood and Jason's heart swelled with feelings so big he had no words to describe them.

He turned on the night-light and grabbed the baby monitor as he left the room in search of Maggie. After giving her an update, he'd go hide in his study and try to get her out of his mind by concentrating on the work he'd brought home.

Next to the nursery, he found her bedroom empty, although looking at her neatly made bed filled him with the need to hold her again. Maybe she was busy in the kitchen. The thought was so completely normal a part of him ached for that to be true. But, in his life, he'd ached for a lot of things that couldn't happen.

"Maggie—" He poked his head in the kitchen and found it empty. Except for his memories. This was where he'd talked to her about the past—about April and his mother.

Maybe Maggie had decided to work out. The last time he'd found her there he'd kissed her. The memory fired his blood like a match within breathing distance of kerosene. Now that he knew what the woman looked like naked, seeing her in workout shorts and tank top would sorely tempt him to separate her from them.

Steeling his self-control for the sight of her on the tread-mill, he opened the door. He wasn't sure whether the empty room or his frustration was more disturbing. Memories of her were everywhere. She'd certainly made her imprint on the penthouse, and quite possibly himself. The only place she hadn't left her mark was his bedroom and if he was smart, he'd go there now to hide. But he needed to let her know the baby was in for the night.

Where the heck was she?

This was different, and a niggling sense of unease trickled through him. He passed the empty living room, then glanced into his office where he saw flickering light. It took several moments to realize candles were lit. And Maggie was there, setting a bottle of wine and two glasses on his desk.

"Maggie?"

She whirled around, her hand to her chest. "Jason—you startled me."

Welcome to the club, he thought, staring at her. Over the faint vanilla scent of the candles, he smelled the floral fragrance that mixed with her skin and was uniquely Maggie. She was barefoot and wearing a strapless cotton sundress. It was a change from the jeans and T-shirt she'd worn at dinner. Her hair was loose, also different from her usual utilitarian ponytail. The dark, shiny, silken strands made his fingers itch to touch.

"I've been looking all over for you."

"You found me." She shrugged and the movement drew his attention to her bare, slender shoulders.

His mouth went dry and he was in serious danger of swallowing his tongue. His acute sexual awareness of her almost kept him from noticing that she looked ill at ease.

"Brady's asleep," he said, setting the baby monitor on his desk.

"He was really tired from our outing at Nooks & Nannies today."

"At the learning center."

She nodded and strands of hair caressed her shoulder. "A

class for babies. The stimulation is geared to this stage of his development to help him learn to feel comfortable, safe and secure in his environment."

One glance at the flimsy elastic holding up her dress sent Jason's environment into stimulation heaven. His brain was still functioning because he got the message loud and clear to escape while he still could.

"Okay, then. I just wanted to let you know he's in for the night and you're off duty." He backed up a step. "I'll say good-night—"

"Wait—" She swallowed and twisted her fingers together. "I mean—well, I was thinking that you might like some wine. With me. Maybe. We could share a glass. Actually, you could even have your own." She laughed nervously. "There's a whole bottle. I opened it just in case."

What was she up to? Stupid question because he had a pretty good idea. It wouldn't be the first time a woman had come on to him, but this was definitely the most inexperienced technique he'd ever encountered. And he found it disconcertingly charming. After the one and only time he'd made love to her, he'd wanted her again within minutes. Every minute since had only increased the need to have her. And this inept, innocent seduction made his need unbearable.

"What are you doing, Maggie?"

"I'm just trying to open the lines of communication between us."

"It won't work." His tone was harsher than he'd intended, but he was running out of places to hide from her. He needed to tap into his inner bastard because he was really starting to question the importance of common sense and nobility.

"The last time I checked, talking was pretty simple," she said.

"If talk was all you wanted, you'd be wearing clothes."

She looked down, then pressed her palms to her yellow-cotton covered midriff, just below her breasts. "These are clothes."

"Not for you. You're the jeans-and-T-shirts type."

"The weather's warmer."

It was definitely warm and not because of the weather. "It's not going to work. I'm not going to take you to bed."

"We're married," she pointed out. "And we've already been down that road. So why not again?"

"If I'd known you were a virgin I'd never have touched you."

"You've made that abundantly clear and it doesn't make any more sense to me now. It's like trying to restore computer data after hitting the Delete button."

"That would be a lot easier." He dragged his fingers through his hair. "Maybe it's a guy thing. But I can't forget that you waited all this time for the right man. That makes you a responsibility. Personal. What we have is strictly business."

"Maybe at first. But remember—as they say on children's programming—walk backward through your mind to the beginning. I fulfilled my part and took care of Brady."

"You do an outstanding job."

"I know. It's not a job because I love him." She smiled tenderly. "You're the one who drew a line in the sand. You're also the first one who crossed it. You kissed me and we tried to ignore that. You crossed your own line again and the kiss led to consummation of our understanding. To me that spells *pattern*. In a married kind of way. So I'm not buying it when you keep playing the business card."

He realized if she hadn't become a nanny, she'd have made a hell of a lawyer. It was imperative to get control of this conversation. "I deliberately structured the agreement to steer clear of emotional considerations. Believe it or not, I'm doing this for you."

"It doesn't feel that way," she said, a bleak expression in her eyes.

"I've tried to forget what happened. I don't want to take advantage of you."

"You didn't," she cried. "That was the best night of my life. The virgin card is off the table. It's no longer an issue."

If only that were true. It made everything even more complicated and she would never understand why. "Just trust me on this, Maggie. Never again. You. Me. Sex. Not happening."

"Wow. Okay. My mistake." If only the embarrassment and humiliation on her face wasn't so easy to read. "I'll just—"

"Maggie—"

She brushed past him and hurried out of the room but not before he saw a tear on her cheek.

"Son of a—" He went after her and caught her in the hall, curving his fingers around her upper arm to stop her. "Please don't cry."

Her back was to him but her shuddering breath was hard to miss. "I'm not crying. I'm not a crier. It's okay. Don't give it another thought. I'm not usually this emotional. Normally everything rolls off my back. I don't know what's wrong with me—"

A sob cut off her words, and he hated that he'd made her cry. He couldn't stand it. He turned her toward him and folded her into his arms. The gesture seemed to break down her control and she buried her face against his chest, her shoulders shaking.

"Don't. I'm not worth it, Maggie."

She looked up. "That's not true, Jason—"

One minute he was looking into her big eyes swimming with tears, the next his mouth was on hers. There was no conscious decision. A deep, primal need took over and he was powerless to resist.

He tasted surprise before her lips parted. His tongue swept inside and took control. The kiss went deeper and he did a quick slide into an all-consuming heat. All he could think about was sinking in further, free-falling with her.

She put her arms around his neck and her small sounds of pleasure made the blood roar in his ears. He scooped her into his arms and carried her down the hall to his bedroom, the last stronghold, the only place her presence hadn't touched.

He stopped by his big king-size, four-poster bed. The sliding-glass door opened onto the penthouse patio and a spectacular view of the lights on the Las Vegas Strip. The brilliance of the neon panorama was no match for the innocent beauty in his arms.

He dropped his arm and let her legs slide down his front. After throwing back the spread and blanket, he looked into her eyes.

He cupped her face in his hands and brushed away the traces of her tears with his thumbs "Are you sure about this, Maggie? Really sure?"

She smiled. "Yes."

That was all he needed to hear to start his heart pounding against the inside of his chest. He let his hands slide into her hair, down her neck and arms. Hooking his thumbs in the top of her dress, he slowly lowered it, revealing her small, perfect breasts.

Sucking in his breath, he held them in his shaking hands and smiled. He hoped he wouldn't wake up and find out, like so many times before, that this was just a dream. "I can't believe how beautiful you are."

She covered his hands with her own, making his touch more secure. "I'm glad you think so."

"I do." And just like that he couldn't wait to see the rest of her.

He tugged on the dress pooled at her waist and pulled it down and over her hips, delighted to learn there was nothing underneath. The rest of her seduction needed work, but she had the most important part down pat.

She reached out and started to unbutton his shirt, but he couldn't wait and brushed her hands aside. After yanking it over his head, he unbuckled his belt and pushed slacks and boxers off until he was as naked as she.

She stepped against him and wrapped her arms around his waist, pressing them skin to skin. The feeling was powerful, passionate and spiked his pulse into the stratosphere.

He backed her against the bed, then gently lowered her to the sheets, settling beside her to kiss her deeply. He trailed his lips down her neck, over her breasts, belly, the inside of her thigh and everywhere else he'd dreamed about.

Slipping a finger inside her, he found that she was wet and waiting and he couldn't hold back any longer. He reached into the nightstand for one of the condoms he kept there and put it on. Then he rose over her and nudged her legs apart with his knee before settling between her thighs.

She took him easily this time and lifted her hands to his chest. "Oh, Jason, you have no idea how much I've wanted this."

She was the one who had no idea. He laughed as he stroked her hair from her face. "Not me. I haven't given it a single thought."

Her innocent eyes went wide. "Really?"

"Only a thousand times a day." He nuzzled her neck. "I've dreamed about you so many times but I always woke with my arms empty."

"Really?" she said, this time with pleasure in her tone.

"Tell me I'm not dreaming now."

She wrapped her legs around his waist and said, "Does that feel like a dream?"

"No," he groaned.

Holding back after that was more than he could manage. He thrust in and pulled back, reaching between their bodies to find the nub of female nerve endings that would give her satisfaction. She sucked in a breath as he lavished attention on the spot. Her breathing became ragged as her hips silently begged for release. An instant later she went still just before her body pulsed with the pleasure pouring through her.

"Oh, my," she said dreamily. "That was the most amazing

feeling I've ever felt." She opened her eyes and smiled. "It was like shattering into a thousand points of light then coming back together."

"I told you the next time would be better," he said.

"And you were right."

She wore the expression of a thoroughly pleased woman and suddenly he couldn't wait to find his own release. He plunged, deeply and gently, over and over, until he felt like his head would explode. A groan came from somewhere deep in his chest and his climax ground through him.

It was the most incredibly satisfying sex he'd ever known, but she had only one experience to compare with. He hoped he'd made it better this time. "Are you okay?"

"I'm perfect." She smiled. "You sure know how to relax a girl."

And those were the words that brought him crashing back to reality. He'd tracked her down and told her to relax because Brady was asleep. Then he'd proceeded to take her to bed and break every vow he'd made to protect her.

She was right about a pattern forming. The thing was, he didn't like the picture it made. And if the future was going to include her being there for his son, he had to find a way to undo what he'd just done.

Chapter Thirteen

"I apologize, Maggie. Hunter and I probably shouldn't have invited ourselves over." Tracy Larson, Hunter Garrett's fiancée, stood by the infant tub on the granite counter in the bathroom and looked over her shoulder. "But I wanted to see the baby."

"It's no problem," Maggie answered. "Brady should get to know his family."

While the men were having after-dinner drinks, the women were bathing Brady. Actually, Tracy was doing the honors under strict supervision and getting soaked when he happily splashed, which didn't seem to bother her. Maggie gave the petite, green-eyed redheaded thirtysomething points for that. She gently dragged a wet washcloth over the baby and, of course, he grabbed it and stuffed the thing in his mouth.

"Brady boo, that's not good for you," Tracy cooed to him. He laughed when she playfully tugged it away, then glanced over her shoulder. "So how's married life?"

Considering that she'd been married for several months,

had sex twice but never actually spent the night in the same bed with her husband, things were just dandy. Maggie's stomach tightened, making nausea that had gripped her the last couple days worse. But she suspected something more than an awkward question was responsible for it. Something that really made her want to throw up.

After making love to her a couple nights ago, Jason had left her alone in the huge four-poster bed and slept on the couch. They'd been as close as a man and woman could be. He'd taken her to a place she'd never gone before. One touch had made her come apart while his arms had kept her together. It had been the best night of her life, then suddenly he was gone, back in his shell and she was more hurt and confused than ever.

"Married life?" she said, tapping her index finger against her lip while leaning a hip against the bathroom vanity. "It's different from the convent."

Tracy laughed and the baby did, too, making them both smile. "Why didn't you take your final vows?"

"I had doubts that the life was right for me." She folded her arms over her chest. "The thought of not ever having a family of my own gave me pause, so Mother Superior advised me to take a leave and think things over."

"And now you're married with a family of your own."

That wasn't exactly true. She was married, but this family was no more hers than the first day she'd walked in the door. Worse, she couldn't imagine loving this baby more if she'd given birth. And Jason? Her feelings for him were complicated. Every time he walked in a room her heart pounded and she couldn't catch her breath. When he wasn't there, it was hard to think about anything but being with him.

"That's a pregnant silence if I ever heard one." Firmly holding on to the baby, Tracy glanced over her shoulder.

If she only knew. "I'm definitely married. And Brady is the sweetest baby in the whole world."

"They're all sweet," Tracy said, longing in her expression when she stared at Brady.

"It's pretty obvious that you like babies." That made Maggie like her. It also made her wonder what Tracy was doing engaged to Jason's father.

"I do love them. I want one desperately and I'm not getting any younger."

"Does Hunter know?"

"Yes." She held out a hand. "Where's the towel? I think the water is getting too cold."

Maggie put the fluffy terry cloth in her fingers, then watched as she put it against her chest and lifted the baby, wrapping him warmly. They walked into the nursery where Tracy diapered him, then massaged his body with cream before putting on a lightweight sleeper.

"Do you mind if I just hold him?" she asked.

"Of course not. And I've got his nighttime bottle ready if he starts to fuss. Feel free to use it."

"Twist my arm."

Tracy sat in the glider chair with Brady in her arms. Almost instantly he began to alternately yawn and whine. This was his routine and he was sticking to it. She offered the bottle and he eagerly took it.

"You seem surprised that I'm a baby person," Tracy observed.

"I guess I am." Maggie remembered the first time she met Hunter, and how he completely ignored his new grandson. It seemed an odd match.

"Did Jason tell you I'm the one who recommended The Nanny Network when he was having problems with reliable child care?"

"No." That was even more surprising.

"My friend Casey Thomas works there."

"We met the other day when I took Brady to a class."

Tracy glanced away from the baby for just a moment. "I

used to date her older brother. We broke up, but I got custody of Casey."

"She doesn't look like she needs taking care of," Maggie commented.

"Don't let that disciplined-soldier exterior fool you."

"Working for The Nanny Network seems like a big change from the army."

Tracy nodded. "She was wounded in Iraq and received a medical discharge. Now she works with kids ten and under."

Maggie thought about her own inclination to care for infants up to six weeks and wondered why Casey specialized in that particular age group. "One of the things I like best about Ginger is her willingness to accommodate an employee's preferences."

"That's Case's feeling, too." Tracy smiled when Brady curled his tiny hand around her finger. "So I sent Jason to Ginger who brought the two of you together. When you think about it, I'm kind of a matchmaker."

"I suppose." Maggie didn't want to answer any more questions about the state of her marriage and decided to change the subject. "So how did you and Hunter meet?"

"I'm a cocktail waitress at the Palms. The Ghost Bar. Hunter came in one night and sparks just flew. He was still married at the time." She looked uncomfortable, but got more points for being honest. "He said he was planning to end the marriage. I know what you're thinking—they all say that."

"My experience is so limited I have no idea what they all say. Actually I was thinking that I respect your honesty."

Tracy's smile was pleased before she grew serious. "Here's a little more for you. If he was still with his wife, I'd continue seeing him. Because I love him."

Maggie didn't know what to say. In her book, that was wrong and love was no excuse. Fortunately she didn't have to comment because the other woman filled in the silence.

"The thing is I do my best to be a realist. I've read the articles—if he cheats with you, he will cheat on you. So, when he proposed, I didn't accept it lightly. Clearly his marital track record makes him a bad risk, but I accept that."

"Why?" Maggie asked.

"Because he makes me happy. And I'll take as much as I can get for as long as I can get it."

"What about children? Does he want a baby?"

"I'm hoping he loves me enough to give me one."

"But what if he doesn't?" If anyone knew how the terms of an agreement changed, it was Maggie.

"I'm not sure. I'll have to cross that bridge when I come to it."

"But what if you're already married and the answer is one you can't live with?"

Tracy frowned before asking a question that actually answered her own. "Did you actually marry Jason expecting happy ever after, Maggie?"

She wasn't sure what to say. Confessing the truth was too awful. Humiliation had been hard enough after taking Ginger's suggestion to argue and fight for a legitimate marriage. Wine, candles and a cotton sundress with nothing underneath had won her an invitation to his bed. Ending up there alone showed her that winning his mind and heart were another story.

Maggie met the other woman's gaze. "My beginning on the steps of the Good Shepherd Home for Children as an infant showed me that there's no such thing as a happy ending."

"It's good you're a realist," Tracy agreed. "Because, like father, like son."

Maggie's chest felt tight. "What do you mean?"

"You shouldn't expect the sun, moon and stars from a man who paid a woman a lot of money not to get rid of his baby."

"What?" Maggie couldn't believe she'd heard right.

"From what Hunter told me Catherine didn't deliberately get pregnant. It was definitely an accident because she's ambitious and determined to make a career in the entertainment business. Pregnancy is good publicity once you're a star, but not so much when you're breaking in. Jason changed her mind with a good-size check."

"I see."

"That's not all. He gave her even more to stay out of Brady's life and not make custody claims later. Rumor has it she's 'having work done.' Eyes, nose, boobs."

So that's what he'd meant when he said Brady's mother wouldn't be an issue. "I'm speechless."

Fortunately Tracy wasn't. As she smiled down at a sleeping Brady, she said, "Can you imagine this precious little life not being here?"

"No."

"I admire Jason for what he did."

So did Maggie. This would all be so much easier if she didn't. She tried not to judge other people lest she be judged. But it was impossible for her to understand how a mother could abandon her child. She would never know what her own mother's reasons were but if Jason weren't rich, Brady wouldn't have had a chance at all.

He bought the baby's life.

He'd bought her life, too.

She'd never thought about it like that before because saving the children's home made her feel as if she was getting the best part of the bargain. But the bargain she'd made didn't work for her now because she wanted Jason's love, not his money.

Looking back, it had probably been love at first sight or she'd never have accepted his unconventional proposal. She'd married a man who understood the power of money but had no clue about people. He had no idea that the same reasons she'd left the convent were even more true now. She wanted a family that included him, Brady, and more children.

She settled her palm protectively against her abdomen and the new life she suspected was growing there. Something that should have been joyous and special made her afraid. He'd made love to her, but if she was pregnant as she suspected, the child hadn't been conceived in love. Jason's actions ever since had proved he meant what he'd told Sister. He wanted no part of a family unit.

He'd simply bought a way out of his child-care problems and was happy with that. But Maggie had never been more unhappy in her life.

Jason looked at his father from where he sat behind the desk in his own study. They were drinking a brandy together, but that didn't mean this wasn't a business meeting. Where Hunter Garrett was concerned, every meeting was business, even a face-to-face with his son. Jason had learned at an early age that it was the only interaction the man understood. No reason to expect anything different now. All he could do was make sure the relationship he had with his own son was different. With Maggie's help it would be.

"So, Dad, when are you and Tracy getting married?"

"I'm in no rush." Hunter took a healthy sip from his glass, then stared into it, frowning thoughtfully. "She wants a baby."

"I kind of figured. What with her wanting to see Brady being the reason for this visit."

"She says her biological clock is ticking."

"And how did you respond to that?" Jason asked.

"Said I didn't hear a thing. She wasn't amused." He shook his head. "I tried everything I can think of to talk her out of it. I'm too old. A baby would tie us down. Was it fair to bring a child into this world in a situation like that?"

"Did you get through to her?"

He sighed. "She said the yearning to have a baby is as strong for a woman as the urge for sex is in a man. That statement was followed by a question about how I'd feel if I couldn't have it ever again."

Jason resisted the urge to squirm. Obviously he knew where babies come from but didn't want the image in his head of Tracy and his father together. He was sorry he'd asked. Although now that he had he was curious.

"How do you feel about it?"

"How would you feel if your current wife wanted another one?" Hunter snapped.

A knot pulled tight in Jason's stomach, but no way was he telling his father about unprotected sex with Maggie. That's where babies come from, but it was only once. Surely his procreation karma couldn't be that messed up. And referring to Maggie as his "current wife" ticked him off.

"Are you planning to marry your *current* fiancée without clarifying the issue?"

Hunter's gaze lifted. "Did I hit a nerve?"

Jason was tempted to blow it off, smooth it over. But he wasn't a kid anymore with one parent left. He was a grown man and he didn't have to worry about what would happen to him if his father left, too.

"Maggie's my wife." She fit seamlessly into his son's life and that's the way he wanted it to stay. He didn't want to hear anything to the contrary. "*Current* implies that there are numerous marriages in my future. I'm not a chip off the old block. I'm not like you."

"Meaning?" Hunter's blue eyes narrowed.

"I don't intend to recycle her like old newspapers. She's one of a kind and I'd be lost without her."

"Don't you mean Brady would be lost?"

Did he? Somehow the line blurred between Brady's needs and how much Jason counted on her being there. "What my relationship is or isn't with Maggie is none of your concern. The point is that I'm happy to follow in your business footsteps. Personal? Not so much. I'd appreciate it if when you talk about my wife, simply use her given name."

Given was definitely the word. Sister Margaret had given her own name to the motherless infant abandoned at her door. She'd given a lot more, molding Maggie into the wonderful, generous, beautiful woman she was today. And Jason realized he could no longer imagine his world without her in it.

Hunter swallowed the remainder of the liquor in his glass, then set it on the desk and applauded. "That was a great speech, Jason. It's easy to make judgments from where you're sitting. For the record, I loved your mother. If she'd stayed, I'd still be with her. It was her idea to leave, not mine. She made the choice."

"Why did she go?" The question popped out and he realized he'd never asked before.

Hunter shrugged. "She gave me some song and dance about obsessive love and not being able to breathe. I gave everything it was in my power to give her and none of it was enough."

Shadows swirled in his father's eyes, stunning him with the implication. He'd thought Hunter Garrett incapable of a deep, lasting love. "I had no idea."

"Now you do." Hunter stood. "And a word to the wise— you may not want to be like me, but you can't escape DNA. I recognize that look."

"What are you talking about?" Jason stood, too, and met his father's gaze.

"You don't defend the nanny unless you have feelings for her. That's a problem, son. I don't want you to get hurt the way I was. Walk away first. Your mother taught me that. If a woman gets your heart, she'll hand it back to you just before setting foot out the door."

He was too surprised to say anything, especially because

the uncharacteristic fatherly advice had come just in time. Defending Maggie had come as easily to Jason as breathing,
proof that his feelings for her were spiraling out of control. It
was time to get a grip.

He heard female voices and no infant crying, which meant
his son was probably asleep. "I think we should join the ladies."

"Okay." Hunter looked at the gold watch on his wrist. "For
a minute. It's time for us to go."

Jason followed his father from the study and into the living
room where Maggie and Tracy were standing in front of the
sliding-glass door that looked out onto the lights of Las Vegas.
The sight of his wife's trim back in her snug-fitting jeans and
cotton blouse stirred his already unsettled emotions. He
missed her when they weren't together and looked forward
to seeing her every night when he came home. And sex had
taken him to a new level of need.

Hunter stopped beside his fiancée and put his arm around
her waist. "So, have you had your fill of the baby experience?"

"He's so adorable," she said, leaning into him.

"Would you like to peek in on him, Mr. Garrett?"
Maggie asked.

"You're my son's wife, *Maggie*." His father glanced at
him. "Call me Hunter."

"All right. Hunter." She looked uneasy. "Brady's asleep but
I'm sure it wouldn't disturb him if you just—"

"We have to get going," the old man said.

Jason knew why he cut her off, but that didn't take the edge
off his own feelings of dismissal and rejection. Brady was the
son of his own son. He and Maggie thought the kid was pretty
damn special, but the old man was running away from his own
problem, one he couldn't buy his way out of. It occurred to
Jason that every marriage since the first one to his mother had
been about Hunter running away.

"Okay." Tracy frowned up at him but chose not to debate.

Her expression said loud and clear that they'd have words about it later. She leaned over and hugged Maggie. "Thanks for letting us drop by."

"Any time," she said warmly.

"Goodbye, Jason. Maggie." Hunter put his hand to Tracy's back, hurrying her to the front door. "I'll be in touch."

That's what Jason said to clients as he ushered them out the door. Damn DNA. Or maybe it was environment. Man, this was a hell of a fix. Without Maggie, he wasn't sure he could break the patterns of his own environment. But given the strong feelings for her he wrestled with day and night, he needed to do something.

When they were alone, he turned to her. "I need to talk to you."

She smiled up at him. "Tracy wants a baby."

"Dad told me."

"She loves him and hopes he loves her enough to give her the one thing she wants most."

Good luck with that, he thought. If Hunter was telling the truth, no woman would ever take his mother's place. He didn't want to find himself in the same position, where no one could replace Maggie.

"I really need to talk with you."

"I was going to make some tea. Would you like some?"

Jason needed something stronger than dried herbs in a bag, but needed to keep his mind clear. "No, thanks."

"Okay."

He followed her to the kitchen, heat radiating through him as he watched the unconsciously sexy sway of her hips. She flipped the lights on and moved confidently around the room, filling a mug with water, then adding the tea before setting it in the microwave. When it was ready, she joined him at the table, sitting at a right angle to him. Lifting her foot to cross her legs, she brushed his calf and he did his best to ignore the arc of electricity that buzzed through him.

"What's up?" she asked.

"It occurs to me that we need to clarify things."

Holding her mug, she blew on the hot water, dispersing the rising steam. "You might want to start with clarifying what you mean by 'things.'"

"Specifically I mean the duration of our arrangement."

Surprise darkened the already vivid blue of her eyes. "We're married. Doesn't that sort of automatically spell it out?"

Clearly she meant that in her world marriage was forever. In his world it didn't work that way and he had to protect himself and his son by making the parameters clear.

"I was thinking that until Brady's in school we should keep things status quo."

"Status quo?" She frowned. "You can't even say married?"

Sometimes her straightforward nature wasn't so appealing, but he'd opened this can of worms. There was no way to unopen it. "He'll be about six, which is about the same age I was when my mother left."

"So what's good for the father is good for the son?"

This was about Brady, not him and his father. "What doesn't kill you makes you stronger. I survived."

"Surviving isn't the same as living a full, rich life." Maggie set her tea on the table and stared at him. "What's wrong, Jason?"

"Who said anything's wrong?"

"Come on. Your father was here and you talked in your office. Now you want to define the duration of our agreement? It doesn't take a Ph.D. in psychology to figure out that he said something to make you go into fight-or-flight mode. Clearly you're choosing the latter."

Anger churned through him, mostly because she knew and understood him so well. How did that happen? When did it? A pointless question that didn't change the fact he wasn't happy about it. "I'm not running away. Just the opposite. It's best for both of us to know where we are with this whole thing."

"'This whole thing' is called marriage and family. You can't even call it what it is. Like they're dirty words." She stood up. "I know where I stand on it. I'm willing to give things between us a fighting chance, but you refuse to risk being happy."

"Maggie, I just want to say—"

"Haven't you already said enough? I've certainly heard enough. Good night, Jason."

When she was gone the kitchen echoed with the silence. It had never seemed so big and empty before Maggie. Would it feel bigger and emptier when "this whole thing" was over? The thought of *his* world without her sweetness in it made him unreasonably angry.

Instead of making things better, he had a very bad feeling that he'd just shot himself in the foot.

Chapter Fourteen

The Saturday following Hunter Garrett's visit, Maggie made a detour on her way to the Good Shepherd Home because a pregnancy test had confirmed her suspicions. If she didn't talk to someone about the situation a personal implosion was entirely possible. Ginger Davis had a penthouse suite in the Trump building located on Fashion Show Drive across from the mall, bordered by Las Vegas Boulevard and Industrial and Desert Inn Roads.

When Maggie drove down Industrial, it occurred to her that the juxtaposition of businesses—Elvis-a-Rama, Love Boutique, and Adult World—with the classy elegance of the tower bearing the famous developer's name was typical of Las Vegas. It was a blend of old and new, good and not so good, the best and worst of life. Right now her life couldn't get much worse.

She found a parking space, then walked into the elegant lobby with its circular marble pattern on the floors, glittery chandeliers, round granite-topped artsy table, wood, glass and mirrors. At the reception desk, she gave her name and was cleared to take the elevator up to the floor where Ginger's suite was located. After exiting, she found the number she was looking for and rang the bell beside the white door with gracefully arched decorative molding.

Since they'd called up from the reception desk, Ginger answered almost immediately. "Maggie, come in."

"Thanks."

She glanced around the foyer and realized she was running out of adjectives. Again, the first word that came to mind was elegant. The floor was beige stone, each tile fitted together with barely a line showing. No grout. Textured paper covered the walls in a seafoam green that was bordered by wide white molding. A large table holding a vase of fresh, sweet-smelling flowers sat in the center.

"Let's talk in the other room," Ginger said, extending her hand.

"I'm sorry to drop in without notice." She followed the other woman into an area with floor-to-ceiling windows and a view of old downtown Vegas.

"Not a problem." Ginger sat on a white, overstuffed loveseat and indicated that Maggie should sit on the one at a right angle, which she did. A rectangular glass-topped table completed the grouping. "What can I do for you?"

"So, you have an office here in your home, too?" Why jump right into a horribly complicated problem when procrastination was so much easier?

"Yes. There's a study in the other room." Ginger glanced around. "I do a lot of computer work here and get together with prospective clients as well as employees. Having the two locations for meetings is convenient for me, too."

"This is a lovely place for a home office."

"I like it very much. And I guess you couldn't help noticing the mall across the street?" Her brown eyes twinkled until the color was like warm maple syrup. "Makes retail therapy incredibly convenient."

Maggie had never been much of a shopper, but could appreciate location, location, location. "It's very beautiful."

"But you didn't come here for a tour. What's bothering you, Maggie?"

She started to question why her former boss would assume there was a problem, but figured that was a waste of time. She had never dropped in like this and any change in habit was a big clue.

"I'm pregnant."

"Congratulations," Ginger said. Then she studied Maggie and frowned. "You're happy about it, right?"

"What was your first clue?"

"It might be sooner than you and Jason planned, but it's the natural next step for a married couple." There was a slight emphasis on the word *married*.

"It couldn't be a worse step for me," Maggie protested.

"I'm sure that's just pregnancy hormones talking. Once you get used to the idea, you'll be ecstatic."

"Do you know how it feels? Have you ever been pregnant?"

A shadow drifted into Ginger's eyes and her smile faltered for a fraction of a second before she restored it. "I've done extensive reading on the subject," she said, not confirming or denying, which was out of character for the straightforward woman. "You love babies, Maggie. Your reputation and experience made you the nanny all new parents requested. There was a waiting list and it was a blow to lose you to Jason Garrett. How can you not want a baby of your own?"

"I never said I didn't want the baby. I've always wanted to be a mother. I just said it couldn't be a worse step for me. Personally. With Jason. Right now," Maggie finished, twisting her fingers together in her lap.

"I don't understand. The marriage was quick, but if anyone understands love at first sight, it's me. Jason isn't the kind of man to take the step without a deeper emotion guiding him."

"It *was* quick," Maggie admitted. "But falling in love? Not so much." At least not for him, but she couldn't say the same for herself. She'd fallen in love with her husband and she was certain of it. All she could think about was being with him. She adored Brady, but when she saw Jason, it was like a light going on in a pitch-black room.

"What's going on?" Ginger slid forward to sit on the edge of the loveseat. "What's the deal, Maggie?"

"Funny you should phrase it like that." She took a deep breath. "He's determined to stick to the finer points of our agreement. Nothing personal."

The other woman's eyes grew large, but she was speechless for several moments. "He's determined to maintain distance even after sleeping with you?"

"Yes. For Brady's sake."

"But you had sex. That's pretty personal. Unless…" If possible her eyes opened wider. "Is Jason the father?"

"What?"

"Did Jason father your baby?"

"Busted," Maggie said. "I picked up a guy while dancing topless at a gentlemen's club. You caught me." She would have laughed at that vision if she wasn't so upset.

"I'm sorry." Ginger shook her head. "This scenario has really thrown me and I'm having trouble wrapping my brain around it."

"Join the club. I was in the convent, for goodness' sake. Nearly a nun. A virgin until that night at the cabin with Jason."

"Let me make sure I understand, so there are no more stupid questions. The marriage was consummated a while ago, before I encouraged you to fight for him," Ginger said.

Maggie nodded. "Although he was trying to go back to the way things were. For the record, I took your advice and it worked out. Temporarily."

"What does that mean?"

"We made love. And then Jason slept on the couch."

"I don't get it." Ginger shook her head again. "He seems like a highly sexual man to me. Obviously he's attracted to you or there wouldn't be a baby."

"He's been hurt and doesn't want to compromise his son's security and stability by giving his heart. He will never let me be more than the nanny."

"Are you sure about that?"

"Very. He's already planning when to sever our relationship." She blew out a breath. "He decided that Brady starting school would be a good time to terminate the agreement and my services as his caregiver will no longer be required."

"He put a time limit on the marriage?" Ginger asked.

"Pretty much."

"Does he know about the baby?"

Maggie shook her head. "I suspected but hadn't confirmed it yet. And when he said we should keep things status quo until Brady's in school, I accused him of going into fight-or-flight mode. Right after that I sort of pointed out that he was afraid to take a chance on being happy."

Ginger nodded her approval. "Good for you."

"Not really. I was pretty harsh. Not that he didn't deserve it, but he's so wounded, Ginger. I just want to help him, and he won't let me."

"Maybe if you tell him about the baby."

"I'm afraid." She met the other woman's gaze. "He has Brady because his girlfriend was going to end her pregnancy and he paid her a lot of money not to do it."

"What does that have to do with you? You're planning to have this baby."

"He gave her a bonus to never darken his door again," Maggie confided. "What if—"

"No." Ginger stared, a fierce expression in her eyes. "This is completely different. I'm not saying there aren't a lot of speed bumps in the road ahead. But you're not that woman. And he married you. He needs to know you're going to have his child."

"I never considered not letting Jason know about the baby."

Ginger smiled. "Of course you didn't. Doing the right thing is your trademark, and Jason knows that, too."

"For what it's worth."

Ginger sighed. "I wish I could give you the magic words or snap my fingers and make everything perfect, but I can't."

Maggie shrugged. "Talking it through helped."

"I believe he cares deeply about you, Maggie. I'm a pretty good judge of character or I wouldn't be a successful businesswoman. If Jason didn't have feelings, he'd never have married you. The question is whether or not he can take a leap of faith and admit how much he cares."

"Jason is capable of great love," Maggie said. "And he's a terrific father. Why wouldn't he love another child, too?"

The bigger question was whether or not he could take a chance on loving her and making a future together. Or if he'd try to make her a nonissue as he'd done with Brady's mother.

Jason sat in a lounge chair on the balcony, the electronic monitor on the glass-topped patio table beside him while Brady was napping. It was a spectacular spring day. Everyone complained about the Vegas heat in July but no one said a bad word when the thermometer hovered just under eighty degrees and there wasn't a cloud in the sky.

His life, on the other hand, had clouds in great quantities and most of them were about Maggie. He looked at the Rolex on his wrist. It was eleven-thirty, which meant she would be walking in the door any minute. Punctuality was one of her best qualities, especially when he'd missed her like crazy. He didn't want to miss her, but couldn't seem to control it.

Even after he'd made such an ass of himself by spelling out the duration of their agreement. What the hell was status quo anyway? He had no idea what was going on with them. She'd called him on it, too. She knew right away it had something to do with his father. Jason could negotiate a business deal until an adversary screamed for mercy but when it came to Maggie he didn't know when to keep his mouth shut. Digging himself in deeper seemed to come naturally when she was around.

You always hurt the ones you love?

The message he grew up with made it tough to know what he was feeling and he'd taken that out on her. He couldn't blame her for walking away first. Even as the words poured out of his mouth, the thought of a life without her in it had his gut tied in knots. Maybe that's why he'd missed her more than usual after she'd left for the children's home yesterday. It also gave him a lot of time to think about how he'd screwed up.

Mostly he was hoping to figure out a strategy to fix things between them. She was trying, and he'd hurt her. He'd loved loving her. He'd loved it too much. And she'd been right when she said that some men would be pleased to be her first, but he'd rejected her.

His only defense was that growing up he'd had no positive role model for a couple's dynamic. He went into every relationship with an exit strategy in mind. It always involved him saying goodbye first, followed by delivery of a very expensive gift. That wouldn't work with Maggie because material things didn't matter to her—people mattered. *He* wanted to matter.

With the patio door opened, Jason heard her come in and felt excitement rush through him. He swung his legs to the side and stood, grabbing the monitor on his way inside.

"Maggie?" He glanced down the hall, toward Brady's room, because that was always her first stop after coming home. It was such a mom thing, he realized and something dark moved in his chest.

She came out of the nursery and pulled the door half-closed behind her. "He's sound asleep. Did everything go all right while I was gone?"

"Fine." Unless she meant his peace of mind. "How are things at Good Shepherd?"

"Oh, you know. Noisy. Chaotic. Wonderful." She twisted her fingers together.

There was a wary, deer-caught-in-headlights look on her face. He didn't like it, or the fact that there was no one to blame but himself. While alone he'd thought a lot about her innocent, awkward attempt at communication while wearing nothing but a simple yellow sundress. His whole body went tense and tight with need, urging him to take her in his arms, kiss her and let his body do the talking. To somehow convey the message that he didn't want her to ever go away again. But that would show weakness and he couldn't shake his core directive not to let her see how much he needed her.

He moved a couple of steps at the same time she did until their bodies were nearly touching. Reaching out, he took a silky strand of her dark hair between his thumb and forefinger.

"Maggie, it's been—"

"There's something I need—"

"Please, ladies first." He dropped his hand. "You go."

"On my way to Good Shepherd I stopped to see Ginger."

"Recruiting reinforcements?" he teased.

She didn't crack a smile, which was disturbing. "She's too busy with The Nanny Network for that."

"Then why did you go there? Looking for work?" The thought that she was planning her own exit strategy had familiar defenses dropping into place to deflect the pain.

"No. I just needed to talk."

He wasn't the poster boy for communication and he knew it. But that didn't keep him from saying, "What am I? Chopped liver?"

"I couldn't talk to you. Not about this."

But she hadn't gone to Sister Margaret. What was it that required a visit to Ginger?

He folded his arms over his chest. "Define *this*."

"I'm pregnant."

His stomach clenched and time stopped. "Pregnant? You're going to have a baby?"

"Yes."

She waited expectantly, but he was too stunned to speak. A baby? She was going to have his baby? He'd tried so hard to maintain stability and keep everything under control. That was laugh-out-loud stupid. With Maggie he'd never been *in* control. The money he'd invested in their agreement had given him the *illusion* of being in charge, but that's all it had been. Otherwise he'd have been able to form coherent thoughts instead of simply wanting her more than his next breath. He'd have been able to think about anything besides the overwhelming need to be with her. Anything including birth control.

Later the reality of what he'd done hit him, but he'd hoped that because it was one time without protection, maybe he wouldn't be punished for just once having what he wanted. This was a hell of a time to find out how high a price he had to pay for that mistake.

"Jason," she pleaded, "please talk to me."

He looked at her and steeled himself against the innocence and uncertainty darkening her eyes. "You're sure?"

She nodded. "I did the test. More than once. It was positive every time. It will be okay. You love Brady so much. I—I hoped you'd be happy about another child."

"Happy?" When he was in defensive mode, anger was his go-to emotion and it didn't fail him now. "That's not even close to what I'm feeling."

She flinched before her chin lifted to meet his gaze. "I know it's unexpected. And we're not what you might call a normal couple. But—"

"In my frame of reference there's no such thing as a 'normal couple.'" This complication was exactly what he'd been afraid of from the beginning.

"Maybe your frame of reference needs work."

He wasn't going there. "So you went to Ginger about this instead of coming to me?"

"Yes." Her look said she refused to apologize for it. "Can you blame me? Our last conversation was about ending this marriage when Brady starts school."

"That might have been a good time to share the news that you were having a baby."

"*We're* having a baby," she said, putting a finer point on the situation.

"What we have is an agreement, a plan, a deal." He saw the hurt in her eyes grow with each word but couldn't seem to stop himself. "That deal was all about you taking care of Brady. It never included giving him a sibling."

Disbelief mixed with distress until her eyes were dark pools of pain. She folded her arms protectively over her abdomen, an instinctively maternal gesture. Finally, without another word, she turned and walked down the hall, then quietly closed the door to her room.

Fuming, Jason walked outside onto the penthouse patio and turned his face into the wind as thoughts raced through his head. Once upon a time he'd craved isolation like this, but that had changed and it was Maggie's fault. Everything else was on him. He wasn't innocent and hadn't been for a very long time. He should have known better.

A baby. Another Brady. Or maybe a girl. Who looked like Maggie.

This was a bad time to realize that her innocence and capacity for caring—all that had attracted him in the first place—were the problem. She didn't understand the concept of the deal. She'd led with her heart. He'd led with his wallet. Until this moment he'd thought money would put him in control of the uncontrollable, the nebulous world of interpersonal relationships. He'd been so sure his "deal" would ensure that he could keep what he wanted most.

Too late he realized his behavior would secure him the highest place in the lowest level of hell. But he wasn't so sure that would be any worse than what he felt right now.

Chapter Fifteen

At four-thirty the next day, Jason walked into the penthouse with his briefcase and a serious case of post-anger confusion. The situation with Maggie hadn't improved. The night before and this morning she'd cared for Brady in her usual tender-loving way. But she hadn't said another word to him. The cruelty of his own words echoed in his head and he'd give anything to be able to go back and delete. There were some things money couldn't buy, and the ability to concentrate while his personal life had gone in the dumper was one of them. Cutting short his day to sort things out seemed prudent.

But when he walked in the living room, Maggie wasn't there with Brady.

"Hello, Jason." Ginger Davis, wearing a navy crepe suit and matching high heels, was on the sofa with the baby in her lap. Brady was all smiles at the sight of him.

"What are you doing here? Where's Maggie?" He walked over and held out his arms for his son.

"Gone." She gave the baby a tender hug before handing him over. "And she called me to cover for her and make sure this little guy was well taken care of."

"Is she sick? She should have called me. I'd have come home to take care of her." He held Brady so close the baby started to squirm. "She knows that."

"Does she?" Ginger tucked a strand of brown hair behind her ear. "From what little she told me, I got the impression that she doesn't feel like she can count on you for anything."

"We've had some minor communication glitches," he hedged.

"Oh, please. It's a marriage, not a computer program."

When Brady fussed, Jason walked back and forth in front of the floor-to-ceiling windows. "Is Maggie all right?"

"Physically?" Ginger leaned back and crossed one trim leg over the other. "She's fine."

"When will she be back?"

"She's not coming back."

"You mean tonight." He nodded. "I'm home now to relieve you. Tomorrow she'll—"

"She's not coming back at all," Ginger clarified. "She quit."

"She can't quit. We're married."

Ginger tilted her head, studying him. "Don't you think it's a little too late to play the *M* card?"

He'd put his briefcase down in the foyer, but his case of confusion had compounded. Instead of answering he said, "When was Brady last changed?"

"I was just about to do that when you walked in."

He nodded, then turned away and carried the baby into the nursery. On the changing table, Brady grabbed the rattle Maggie always kept there to keep his little hands busy. "Hey, buddy. How was your day? I bet you're pretty mixed up. Join the club."

"Is it really that big a stunner, Jason?"

He glanced over his shoulder to see Ginger standing in the doorway. "Of course I'm surprised. I had nanny trouble when he was first born, which is why I hired your agency. It came highly recommended. Now I'm not so sure."

"Are you put out because you lost a nanny? Or is this shock and awe about your *wife* walking out on you? Pick one because you can't have it both ways."

It would be so much easier to make it about an employee. The first three nannies hadn't crossed his mind since he'd let them go. But Maggie hadn't been out of his mind since the first time he'd seen her.

He finished diapering Brady and snapping his overalls, then put his palm on the baby's belly to keep him secure as he faced the woman. "Do you know why she left?"

"Yes." Ginger folded her arms over her chest.

He waited but she didn't say more. "Are you going to tell me?"

"Do you really want to know?"

"Of course I do."

"Why?"

He picked Brady up and said the first thing that came to mind. "Because this is out of character for her. She takes responsibility seriously. She's organized and conscientious and she loves Brady. Why would she do this?"

"She loves that little boy more than her life, but the cost of loving you is her soul. Don't you think that's an awfully high price to pay?"

He was stunned. Maggie loved him? "She told you that?"

"Pretty much." Ginger's expression hardened. "And before you claim this is news to you, she also told me she's pregnant. And you were less than thrilled."

He put a thick quilt on the floor and set Brady down with toys. "Did she also mention that the Garrett men have a lousy track record with women?"

"She didn't have to. Your father makes the 'Vegas Confidential' column on a regular basis. And I knew your mother."

He straightened and stared at her. "When?"

"Right after she left your father." Ginger leaned against the baby's crib. "We both worked the registration desk at one of the Strip hotels. It was just one of her jobs. She was working three."

"Why?"

"Trying to earn enough money for the legal battle to get you back."

"But she walked out on me."

Ginger shook her head. "No. She walked out on your father when her life with him became intolerable. He refused to let her take you. She spent time with you when she could, but knew that with all Hunter's money, a court fight for custody would be a joke without a sizable bank account of her own."

"Did my dad know?" He'd certainly never shared the information if he did.

"I'm not sure. Your mom was a smart cookie and it wouldn't have been very intelligent to give him a heads-up." She looked down for a moment, sadness in her expression. "Unfortunately she was killed in a car accident before she could follow through on her plan."

"Dad told me about the accident, but not that she wanted me to go with her when she left." Something shifted in his chest. Something dark and heavy broke free and slipped away.

"I'm not surprised." She shrugged. "Your father isn't the sort of man who'd share how much your mother loved you. That wouldn't be a win for him."

"Yeah." He watched Brady roll from his tummy to his back and wave his arms. "I got the version about him giving her everything, including his love and it wasn't enough for her."

"She loved him once. And he probably loved her in his way," Ginger said. "But his way included holding on to her so tightly that he squeezed every last drop of love out of her. It was oppressive. He was so afraid of losing her, he all but pushed her out the door."

"And he keeps making the same mistakes."

"At least he's not shutting himself off."

Now she was defending Hunter? "You can't have it both ways, Ginger. Is he a bastard or not?"

"Your mother was the love of his life and your father's string of relationships are about looking for that feeling again." Ginger took a step forward. "He lost your mother because he held on too tightly. You lost Maggie because you won't hold on at all."

"Wait a minute—"

"Don't get me wrong. I'm the last one to defend Hunter Garrett, but at least your father isn't hiding under a rock. He keeps getting it wrong, but he hasn't given up. Unlike you."

She was comparing him to his father? Now she'd crossed a line.

"Hold it. You don't know me. What gives you the right to judge me? I'm not my father." He settled his hands on his hips. "Maggie and I have an understanding. I was honest with her, as straight with her as I know how to be. I gave her everything she needed—"

"Everything but what she needed most." Intensity darkened her eyes.

"What did she need that I didn't give?"

"Yourself." She put her hand on his arm. "Think about it, Jason. She married you to save the home that saved her and Good Shepherd became her family by default. All she's ever wanted was a family of her own, freely given because of love. Do you have any idea how precious that is to her?"

Her words were like pulling the plug on his anger and it all drained away, leaving him nowhere left to hide. "I don't want Maggie to go away. Do you know where she is?"

"Yes."

"Tell me. Please," he added.

"You want her to come back?" Ginger asked.

"Of course I do."

"Why?"

Hadn't they just been through this? What the hell was she doing? "Brady misses her."

Ginger actually smiled. "He told you that?"

"He didn't have to. She's the only mother he knows. Not having her here will confuse him."

"I think you and I know who's really confused. Trust me. I've been around the block a time or two. You'll feel a whole lot better if you just tell me why you want Maggie back."

For a man who thrived on fixing things, all this conversation seemed like a waste of time and energy. Every part of him vibrated with the need to see Maggie, to talk to *her*. To negotiate terms for her return, probably including an apology if he could find the right words. First he needed to know where she'd gone and to get that information he had to pass some test of Ginger's.

"Why do I want Maggie back?" He raked his fingers through his hair. "Because I need her. She makes everything better. She makes me better. I can't imagine my life without her in it. She's the best thing that ever happened to me."

"You love her."

"I care very much for her."

Ginger shook her head, pity in the gesture. "Why is it so hard to say the *L* word?"

"Because I don't want to screw things up like my father." He curled his fingers into his palms. "Where is she?"

"She's home. With her family."

Good Shepherd. Of course.

"I have to see her. Will you—"

"Stay with Brady?" She nodded. "You don't even have to ask. Go get his mother."

"Yes, ma'am."

She pointed at him. "Smile when you call me that."

He grinned before saluting, then raced out of the pent-house. Before seeing Maggie he had a stop to make: Until now, he'd always gone into a relationship with an exit strategy in mind. This time he needed an entrance plan. Until now, walking away included an expensive present. This time he needed something that would show Maggie he loved her and was in this relationship forever.

When the kids at the home had finished eating and the kitchen was tidied, Maggie went to the little room nearby that served as Sister Margaret's office. She knocked softly on the door and when she heard "come in," she did. Sister was behind her desk, reading glasses on the end of her nose as she squint-ed at a computer monitor.

"Sister Mary said you wanted to see me?"

"Yes." The nun smiled. "Sit down, Maggie."

There was a generic visitor's chair in front of the desk and she sat. "What's up?"

"You tell me."

"I don't understand."

"Yes, you do. While I personally don't believe a lie that small will keep you out of heaven, stalling is counterproduc-tive." Sister removed her glasses and looked across the space with eyes that had never missed anything. "It's not Saturday. You take care of Jason's son the rest of the week. Who's watching him because you ran away?"

"He's in good hands," she said. "I needed a break."

"Why?"

Because Jason didn't want her or the baby they'd made together. Between the punch of that thought and the pain that always followed, there was a blessed numbness she tried des-perately to hold on to. It lasted a nanosecond before tears burned the backs of her eyes. There was no point in pretend-ing. She'd never been able to fool Sister Margaret.

"I'm pregnant."

Sister's eyes widened a fraction but it was the only indication that she was surprised. "I see. An out-of-wedlock pregnancy—"

"It's not out of wedlock." Maggie sat on the edge of the chair. "Jason and I are married."

This time Sister couldn't suppress her shock. "You're married? When?"

"Six weeks after I went to work for him. He didn't want me to leave."

"A man of action who fell in love and—"

"No." Maggie hated to destroy Sister's romantic fantasy. "He wanted me to take care of Brady. When I shared my reasons for limiting my stay, he offered marriage as a solution that would work for both of us."

"I see."

"That's not all."

"Good gracious, Margaret Mary. What more can there be?"

"I turned down his offer."

"But you say you're married." Sister Margaret looked confused. "I don't understand."

This part was the hardest because she didn't want Sister to blame herself in any way. "He—Jason—was raised by his father to believe that money buys a way out of problems. If you want something badly enough, you simply have to find the right number to put on a check."

"And?"

"When I told him Good Shepherd was in trouble because the building was in disrepair, he offered me a million dollars to marry him."

"Oh, Maggie, no—"

"It was a chance to give back when I'd received so much," she hurried to explain. The words kept rushing out. "I just couldn't stand the thought of Lyssa and the other kids losing their home. If not for Good Shepherd I'd have had no one, nothing. It felt like the right thing to do. At the time."

"And now?" Sister asked.

"Now everything is all wrong." Her lips trembled. "I thought he cared when we were—he seemed so caring when the two of us—you know."

"Made love?"

"Yes," she said, relieved that Sister said it for her.

"Does he know about the baby?"

"I told him."

"Since I know you so well, it's not necessary to ask if you have feelings for him. There wouldn't be a baby if you didn't. That means you're here because he doesn't have feelings for you. Is that right?"

"He won't let himself care." A single tear slipped down her cheek.

Sister stood and came around the desk, pulling Maggie to her feet for one of the comforting hugs she remembered. She hung on for all she was worth and let the tears come while Sister patted her back and murmured words of encouragement until Maggie pulled away, swiping at the moisture on her cheeks.

"Don't cry, Margaret Mary." Sister's expression was full of sympathetic wisdom. "I know it seems hopeless right at this moment. But remember what I used to tell you when you were a little girl? God always does things right, even if it seems wrong to us."

"But I don't know what I'm going to do."

"That's all right. You can be sure He will give you what you need at the appropriate time."

Maggie had told Lyssa the same thing, but right at this moment it was very hard to believe.

There was a knock on the door and Sister looked at Maggie, asking with a look if she was okay. Maggie nodded and she said, "Come in."

"Hi, Sister." It was Rachel, a slender, dark-haired sixteen-year-old who lived at the home. "Hey, Maggie. There's a guy at the door. Says he wants to see you."

Jason. She didn't know any other guy, let alone one who would look for her here. She couldn't face him like this. "Sister, I don't want to see him."

"You can't run away from this forever, Maggie." The nun glanced down at her flat abdomen.

"I know. And I won't. But I need a little time before I face him again." From the hall a man's familiar voice drifted through the open door. "Please run interference for me, Sister. I'm going in the other room."

"All right." Sister nodded and Maggie quickly slipped into the adjoining room. She heard the nun say, "Show the gentleman in."

With the connecting door open, Maggie could hear Jason as if he were standing in front of her. His deep, velvety voice wrapped around her like a warm blanket and raised tingles over her skin.

"Sister," he said, "it's nice to see you again."

"I wish I could say the same."

"Maggie told you?"

"Everything, yes."

"Where is she?" he asked. "I have to talk to her."

"She doesn't want to see you, Mr. Garrett. It's not an exaggeration to say that you didn't take the news of the pregnancy well."

"No."

In the brief silence Maggie pictured him raking his fingers through his wonderful thick hair as he always did when he was uncomfortable.

Jason cleared his throat. "I don't think anyone will argue when I say that I handled the situation with all the sensitivity of a water buffalo."

"At least you admit your failing."

"As lame as it sounds, I can only say in my own defense that the news about the baby came as a shock."

"That makes two of us," Sister said wryly, making Maggie squirm again.

"I hurt her. If I could, I'd take it back in a heartbeat. Hurting Maggie is the last thing in the world I would ever want to do. I need to see her. Tell me where she is."

"I can't," Sister said firmly.

"I have to make things right between us. She needs to know how wrong I was about everything. I have to apologize and somehow convince her to forgive me. Tell her I'm here. Please."

There was a note of intensity in his voice, bordering on desperation, Maggie thought. This didn't sound like the cool and controlled Jason she knew. This was more like the man who'd kissed her because he couldn't seem to help himself.

"I'm sorry, Mr. Garrett. She made it absolutely clear that she doesn't want to see you. When all is said and done, Maggie is a girl who believes in God, prayer and marriage forever. Apparently you don't share her convictions."

"What can I do to convince you that I'm not here to hurt her? I want to make it right."

"Why is it so important?"

"Because I'm in love with her."

Maggie stood up straight, away from the wall. She'd expected him to pull out his checkbook, so his declaration got her attention in a big way. There was what could only be described as a pregnant silence in the other room.

Finally, Sister said, "Maggie, come in here please."

With her stomach quivering in a way that had nothing to do with the baby and everything to do with Jason, Maggie stepped into the room. Jason looked uncharacteristically rumpled and completely wonderful with the long sleeves of his white dress shirt rolled up and his red tie loosened at the collar. Expertly tailored gray slacks hugged his flat abdomen and muscular legs. He was a sight for eyes aching from the tears she'd cried just moments ago.

"Hello," she said.

"Maggie, I—"

"I don't mind saying that this situation is beyond my sphere of expertise," Sister said. "I'm going to leave you to sort this out."

Before Maggie could protest, the door closed and she was alone with him. She said the first thing that popped into her head. "How's Brady?"

"Fine. He seems happy with Ginger. But not as happy as he is with you." He frowned. "It's not like you to run away from a situation. Why did you leave?"

"Because, as it turns out, I can't live up to the deal I made. I can't stay because my heart breaks a little more every day, knowing you'll never feel about me the way I do about you." She twisted her hands together. "I'll pay you back the money. Somehow. If you'll give me some time."

He shook his head as already dark eyes darkened even more. "The rest of my life won't be enough time."

"I know it's a lot of money, but—"

"You don't understand, Maggie." He moved forward and stood right in front of her without touching. "I love you. I'm in love with you. The rest of my life won't be enough time to make up for the hurt I've caused. I feel like I've waited an eternity for you and a lifetime isn't long enough to love you."

"I know it's a lot, but—"

He touched a finger to her lips. "The cost of having my son was losing my faith in people." He looked around the tiny office. "Repairs to Good Shepherd cost me a measly million. Falling in love with you is priceless."

She shook her head even as hope filled her heart. "Why should I believe you now? How do I know you want what I do? Like Sister said, I'm a girl who believes in God, the power of prayer and until-death-shall-part-us marriage. Ours is based on a cash transaction. All I am is an asset to you."

Jason shook his head. "One doesn't care about an asset the way I care about you. You don't miss the scent of an asset when she's gone. An asset doesn't determine whether every heartbeat will be full of joy or unbearable pain. No matter how hard I tried, I couldn't seem to make you an asset." A fierce intensity glowed in his eyes. "And I didn't know you were in the next room when I told Sister Margaret how I feel. If you don't believe anything else, you have to believe I'd never lie to a nun." He drew in a deep, shuddering breath. "And I'll never lie to you. The church's loss is my gain. I am incredibly grateful that you didn't become a nun."

"Jason, you're a good man. I know that, but—"

"No buts." He reached into his pocket and pulled out a small, black velvet jeweler's box, and flipped it open. "You're beautiful and good and the woman most likely not to get caught up in material things. But I'm hoping just this once you'll make an exception." Uncertainty trickled into his normally confident gaze. "Before you, I went into a relationship always formulating my strategy to get out first. I made mental notes to personalize the outrageously expensive gift that would take the sting out of breaking things off with a woman. Not this time."

She looked at the ring—a round diamond solitaire in a platinum band. "What does this mean?"

"I want a relationship with you for the rest of our lives. This is my entrance strategy." He got down on one knee. "Margaret Mary Shepherd, will you marry me?"

"But we're already married."

"Not in the church. We'll do it right this time." He cocked his thumb over his shoulder, indicating the home where she grew up. "We'll have a big wedding with your family there. I'll beg if I have to." He put his palm on her abdomen. "I want this baby. With you. There's nothing more important to me than family. And Brady needs you—his mom."

Joy filled her, making her lightheaded. It was hard to believe he was offering her everything she'd ever wanted.

She put her hands on his shoulders and stared into his eyes. The first time she'd met him he'd tried to conduct an interview and it was time to return the favor. "As it happens, I'm interviewing for a husband. I'd very much like to see your résumé. You can messenger it over."

He stood, grinning the grin that had stolen her heart the day she met him. Folding her in his arms, he said, "I can do better than that."

He lowered his mouth to hers and kissed her until her legs threatened to buckle. When he lifted his head, he met her gaze, his own filled with nobility, sincerity and love.

"I promise to be a good father and an exemplary husband. I love you," he said simply.

"You're hired," she said, "because I love you more."

"Not possible."

"Oh, yes it is." She stood on tiptoe, pressed her lips to his, savoring the sweetness of this negotiating technique.

No longer the virgin nanny, Maggie was happier than she'd ever thought to be. She was loved and in love with a wonderful man. She was a wife and mother with a family of her very own and it was everything she'd ever hoped for.

* * * * *

*Celebrate 60 years of pure reading pleasure with Harlequin®!
Silhouette® Romantic Suspense is celebrating with the
glamour-filled, adrenaline-charged series LOVE IN 60
SECONDS starting in April 2009.
Six stories that promise to bring the glitz of Las Vegas, the
danger of revenge, the mystery of a missing diamond,
family scandals and ripped-from-the-headlines intrigue.
Get your heart racing as love happens in sixty seconds!*

Enjoy a sneak peek of
USA TODAY *bestselling author Marie Ferrarella's*
THE HEIRESS'S 2-WEEK AFFAIR
Available April 2009 from Silhouette® Romantic Suspense.

Eight years ago Matt Shaffer had vanished out of Natalie Rothchild's life, leaving behind a one-line note tucked under a pillow that had grown cold: *I'm sorry, but this just isn't going to work.*

That was it. No explanation, no real indication of remorse. The note had been as clinical and compassionless as an eviction notice, which, in effect, it had been, Natalie thought as she navigated through the morning traffic. Matt had written the note to evict her from his life.

She'd spent the next two weeks crying, breaking down without warning as she walked down the street, or as she sat staring at a meal she couldn't bring herself to eat.

Candace, she remembered with a bittersweet pang, had tried to get her to go clubbing in order to get her to forget about Matt.

She'd turned her twin down, but she did get her act

together. If Matt didn't think enough of their relationship to try to contact her, to try to make her understand why he'd changed so radically from lover to stranger, then to hell with him. He was dead to her, she resolved. And he'd remained that way.

Until twenty minutes ago.

The adrenaline in her veins kept mounting.

Natalie focused on her driving. Vegas in the daylight wasn't nearly as alluring, as magical and glitzy as it was after dark. Like an aging woman best seen in soft lighting, Vegas's imperfections were all visible in the daylight. Natalie supposed that was why people like her sister didn't like to get up until noon. They lived for the night.

Except that Candace could no longer do that.

The thought brought a fresh, sharp ache with it.

"Damn it, Candy, what a waste," Natalie murmured under her breath.

She pulled up before the Janus casino. One of the three valets currently on duty came to life and made a beeline for her vehicle.

"Welcome to the Janus," the young attendant said cheerfully as he opened her door with a flourish.

"We'll see," she replied solemnly.

As he pulled away with her car, Natalie looked up at the casino's logo. Janus was the Roman god with two faces, one pointed toward the past, the other facing the future. It struck her as rather ironic, given what she was doing here, seeking out someone from her past in order to get answers so that the future could be settled.

The moment she entered the casino, the Vegas phenomena took hold. It was like stepping into a world where time did not matter or even make an appearance. There was only a sense of "now."

Because in Natalie's experience she'd discovered that bartenders knew the inner workings of any establishment they worked for better than anyone else, she made her way to the first bar she saw within the casino.

The bartender in attendance was a gregarious man in his early forties. He had a quick, sexy smile, which was probably one of the main reasons he'd been hired. His name tag identified him as Kevin.

Moving to her end of the bar, Kevin asked, "What'll it be, pretty lady?"

"Information." She saw a dubious look cross his brow. To counter that, she took out her badge. Granted she wasn't here in an official capacity, but Kevin didn't need to know that. "Were you on duty last night?"

Kevin began to wipe the gleaming black surface of the bar. "You mean during the gala?"

"Yes."

The smile gracing his lips was a satisfied one. Last night had obviously been profitable for him, she judged. "I caught an extra shift."

She took out Candace's photograph and carefully placed it on the bar. "Did you happen to see this woman there?"

The bartender glanced at the picture. Mild interest turned to recognition. "You mean Candace Rothchild? Yeah, she was here, loud and brassy as always. But not for long," he added, looking rather disappointed. There was always a circus when Candace was around, Natalie thought. "She and the boss had at it and then he had our head of security escort her out."

She latched onto the first part of his statement. "They argued? About what?"

He shook his head. "Couldn't tell you. Too far away for anything but body language," he confessed.

"And the head of security?" she asked.

"He got her to leave."

She leaned in over the bar. "Tell me about him."

"Don't know much," the bartender admitted. "Just that his

name's Matt Shaffer. Boss flew him in from L.A., where he was head of security for Montgomery Enterprises."

There was no avoiding it, she thought darkly. She was going to have to talk to Matt. The thought left her cold. "Do you know where I can find him right now?"

Kevin glanced at his watch. "He should be in his office. On the second floor, toward the rear." He gave her the numbers of the rooms where the monitors that kept watch over the casino guests as they tried their luck against the house were located.

Taking out a twenty, she placed it on the bar. "Thanks for your help."

Kevin slipped the bill into his vest pocket. "Any time, lovely lady," he called after her. "Any time."

She debated going up the stairs, then decided on the elevator. The car that took her up to the second floor was empty. Natalie stepped out of the elevator, looked around to get her bearings and then walked toward the rear of the floor.

"Into the Valley of Death rode the six hundred," she silently recited, digging deep for a line from a poem by Tennyson. Wrapping her hand around a brass handle, she opened one of the glass doors and walked in.

The woman whose desk was closest to the door looked up. "You can't come in here. This is a restricted area."

Natalie already had her ID in her hand and held it up. "I'm looking for Matt Shaffer," she told the woman.

God, even saying his name made her mouth go dry. She was supposed to be over him, to have moved on with her life. What happened?

The woman began to answer her. "He's—"

"Right here."

The deep voice came from behind her. Natalie felt every single nerve ending go on tactical alert at the same moment that all the hairs at the back of her neck stood up. Eight years had passed, but she would have recognized his voice anywhere.

* * * * *

*Why did Matt Shaffer leave heiress-turned-cop Natalie
Rothchild?
What does he know about the death of Natalie's twin sister?
Come and meet these two reunited lovers and learn the
secrets of the Rothchild family in
THE HEIRESS'S 2-WEEK AFFAIR
by USA TODAY bestselling author
Marie Ferrarella.
The first book in Silhouette® Romantic Suspense's wildly
romantic new continuity,
LOVE IN 60 SECONDS!
Available April 2009.*

CELEBRATE
60 YEARS
OF PURE READING PLEASURE
WITH HARLEQUIN®!

Look for Silhouette®
Romantic Suspense in April!

Love In 60 Seconds

Bright lights. Big city. Hearts in overdrive.

Silhouette® Romantic Suspense is celebrating Harlequin's 60th Anniversary with six stories that promise to bring readers the glitz of Las Vegas, the danger of revenge, the mystery of a missing diamond, and family scandals.

**Look for the first title, *The Heiress's 2-Week Affair*
by *USA TODAY* bestselling author
Marie Ferrarella, on sale in April!**

---

www.eHarlequin.com   SRS60BPA

Undone!

THE RAKE'S INHERITED COURTESAN
Ann Lethbridge

Christopher Evernden has been assigned the unfortunate task of minding Parisian courtesan Sylvia Boisette. When Syliva sets off to find her father, Christopher has no choice but to follow and finds her kidnapped by an Irishman. Once rescued, they finally succumb to the temptation that has been brewing between them. But can they see past the limitations such a love can bring?

Available April 2009
wherever books are sold.

REQUEST YOUR FREE BOOKS!
2 FREE NOVELS PLUS 2 FREE GIFTS!

SPECIAL EDITION®

Life, Love and Family!

YES! Please send me 2 FREE Silhouette Special Edition® novels and my 2 FREE gifts (gifts are worth about $10). After receiving them, if I don't wish to receive any more books, I can return the shipping statement marked "cancel." If I don't cancel, I will receive 6 brand-new novels every month and be billed just $4.24 per book in the U.S. or $4.99 per book in Canada, plus 25¢ shipping and handling per book and applicable taxes, if any*. That's a savings of at least 15% off the cover price! I understand that accepting the 2 free books and gifts places me under no obligation to buy anything. I can always return a shipment and cancel at any time. Even if I never buy another book from Silhouette, the two free books and gifts are mine to keep forever.

235 SDN EEYU   335 SDN EEY6

Name	(PLEASE PRINT)	
Address		Apt. #
City	State/Prov.	Zip/Postal Code

Signature (if under 18, a parent or guardian must sign)

Mail to the Silhouette Reader Service:
IN U.S.A.: P.O. Box 1867, Buffalo, NY 14240-1867
IN CANADA: P.O. Box 609, Fort Erie, Ontario L2A 5X3

Not valid to current subscribers of Silhouette Special Edition books.

Want to try two free books from another line?
Call 1-800-873-8635 or visit www.morefreebooks.com.

* Terms and prices subject to change without notice. N.Y. residents add applicable sales tax. Canadian residents will be charged applicable provincial taxes and GST. Offer not valid in Quebec. This offer is limited to one order per household. All orders subject to approval. Credit or debit balances in a customer's account(s) may be offset by any other outstanding balance owed by or to the customer. Please allow 4 to 6 weeks for delivery. Offer available while quantities last.

Your Privacy: Silhouette is committed to protecting your privacy. Our Privacy Policy is available online at www.eHarlequin.com or upon request from the Reader Service. From time to time we make our lists of customers available to reputable third parties who may have a product or service of interest to you. If you would prefer we not share your name and address, please check here. ☐

SSE08R

The Inside Romance newsletter has a NEW look for the new year!

Same great content, brand-new look!

The Inside Romance newsletter is a FREE quarterly newsletter highlighting our upcoming series releases and promotions!

Click on the Inside Romance link on the front page of **www.eHarlequin.com** or e-mail us at insideromance@harlequin.ca to sign up to receive your FREE newsletter today!

You can also subscribe by writing to us at: HARLEQUIN BOOKS Attention: Customer Service Department P.O. Box 9057, Buffalo, NY 14269-9057

Please allow 4-6 weeks for delivery of the first issue by mail.

IRNNEW09

Silhouette®

COMING NEXT MONTH
Available March 31, 2009

SPECIAL EDITION®

#1963 THE BRAVO BACHELOR—Christine Rimmer
Bravo Family Ties
For attorney Gabe Bravo, sweet-talking young widow
Mary Hofstetter into selling her ranch to BravoCorp should have
been a cinch. But the stubborn mom turned the tables and got him
to bargain away his bachelorhood instead!

#1964 A REAL LIVE COWBOY—Judy Duarte
Fortunes of Texas: Return to Red Rock
CEO William "J.R." Fortune gave up the L.A. fast life to pursue
his dream of becoming a Texas rancher. Luckily, hiring decorator
and Red Rock native Isabella Mendoza to spruce up his new spread
ensured he'd get a very warm welcome in his brand-new life!

#1965 A WEAVER WEDDING—Allison Leigh
Famous Families
A one-night stand with Axel Clay left Tara Browning pregnant.
But when she was forced to share very close quarters with the sexy
bodyguard, would she end up with a love to last a lifetime?

#1966 HEALING THE M.D.'S HEART—Nicole Foster
The Brothers of Rancho Pintada
To help his sick son, Duran Forrester would do anything—including
a road trip to Rancho Pintada to find the long-lost family who might
hold the key to a cure. But first, he crossed paths with pediatrician
Lia Kerrigan, who had a little TLC for father and son alike….

**#1967 THE RANCHER & THE RELUCTANT PRINCESS—
Christine Flynn**
After her unscripted remarks blew up in the tabloids, Princess Sophie
of Valdovia needed to cool off out of the public eye in middle-of-
nowhere Montana. But that's where things heated up—royally—with
rancher and single dad Carter McLeod….

#1968 THE FAMILY HE WANTED—Karen Sandler
Fostering Family
Bestselling novelist Sam Harrison had it all—so why did the former
foster kid-made-good feel so empty inside? The answer came when
old friend Jana McPartland showed up on his porch, pregnant and in
distress, and he realized that it was family he wanted…and family he
was about to find.

SSECNMBPA0309